PATHS TO MOTHERHOOD

JOURNEYS THROUGH INFERTILITY & PREGNANCY LOSS

EDITED BY KATHERINE HUNTER

FOREWORD BY LAUREN MANAKER

First paperback edition August 2021.

Front and back cover design by HAREYRA

Imagery by Robin J. Marquand

ISBN: 978-0-578-93452-5

Published by Katherine Hunter

pathstomotherhood@gmail.com

Dedication

To the women whose paths to motherhood are full of unexpected and arduous twists and turns, detours, and roadblocks: we see you. This book is for you.

"Hope is the thing with feathers that perches in the soul—and sings the tunes without the words—and never stops at all."

— ***Emily Dickinson***

"Walking with a friend in the dark is better than walking alone in the light."

— ***Helen Keller***

"Don't confuse your path with your destination. Just because it's stormy now doesn't mean you aren't headed for sunshine."

— ***Anonymous***

Contents

Foreword

If you are reading this book, you may very well be a part of the "fertility warrior" club. It took my husband and me five years of trying everything under the sun to become parents. And after a lot of needles, tears, and money, we finally welcomed our baby girl in 2015.

I know I was not alone in feeling isolated, scared, and frustrated during my journey to motherhood. As a fertility-focused registered dietitian, I have worked with many people struggling to become (and sometimes stay) pregnant. Through my own infertility experience and by observing the experiences of my patients, I have witnessed the success a fertility-supporting diet (and lifestyle), and medical interventions in certain situations, can yield. And I have also witnessed (including first-hand) how utterly therapeutic and motivating it can be to hear others' stories while in the trenches of infertility. During my infertility journey, I found myself connecting with friends of friends and hearing their stories. It would have been so comforting to have had a handful of experiences right at my fingertips as you have right now.

When I learned that Katherine was creating this book, I thought it was a brilliant idea. While there are many nutritional and medical resources out there geared toward helping people on their journey to motherhood, there aren't many resources that offer emotional support—and there is a lot of emotion that goes into this journey.

Reading the stories in this book will help make you feel less alone. There is comfort in knowing that you are not the only one who has experienced these challenges. And learning about the successful outcomes will undoubtedly give you some hope for reaching the light at the end of the tunnel.

Katherine herself bravely shares her story, which is relatable, heartbreaking, and joyful—essentially a similar emotional roller coaster that you may be riding currently. Reading her story—along with the others' stories—is like having friends intimately share their stories while sipping a glass of wine.

Katherine's effort to collect these stories was undoubtedly a labor of love, and having these stories at your fingertips is a true blessing. I wish you all of the baby dust in the world. And I hope that reading these stories will bring you the peace and comfort you need.

Warmly,

Lauren Manaker MS, RDN, LD, CLEC, CPT
-Fertility and Prenatal Registered Dietitian, Book Author, and Fertility Advocate

Introduction

I don't know the genesis of human storytelling, but I do know humans have been telling stories for a very long time. Storytelling, whether in oral or written form, is undeniably powerful. Many would argue that complex and paramount human constructs, such as politics and religion, could not exist without human storytelling. Over time, a story may have the ability to transform humanity in a monumental way, on a macro level. And stories, such as the ones that comprise this book, can also create community, soothe the human spirit, elevate an individual's self-worth, unearth hidden desires, illicit empathy, and inspire the reader (or listener) to act.

When I experienced my first miscarriage in 2013, I went searching for stories. I was desperate to find others' stories about pregnancy loss. No one close to me had experienced a miscarriage (absent my mother 30 years earlier). And even if I had known someone who had experienced a miscarriage, I may still have felt too vulnerable to confide in them about my loss. So, I scoured the internet in search of stories about other women's experiences. I wanted to know what a miscarriage entailed, both physically and emotionally. I also craved the solace that reading a personal story by a mere stranger could provide. I wanted to feel less alone. I wanted to feel that, in some sense, I had someone holding my hand, guiding me down the path of loss (and later, infertility), and offering a form of comfort.

I found very little support. I remember watching a video clip on YouTube of Beyonce talking about her miscarriage. I felt some sense of relief in hearing her speak, knowing I was not alone. I also found a blogger's post about her miscarriage. Her words helped prepare me for what would ensue, although I wished she had spared no details. I wanted to know more.

I felt too vulnerable during my infertility journey to share my struggles publicly. I did write a blog, and some posts were about my infertility struggles, but I kept the blog private for quite some time and was judicious about with whom I shared it. I felt ashamed about my inability to get pregnant easily and stay pregnant. I felt like a failure. I did not want to take others along for the ride through the hellish labyrinth I was navigating, both because I was not adept at the navigation and because I did not want to feel obligated to keep providing updates on my failures. While I could not muster the courage to share my journey publicly, I knew that if I ever did become a mother I would want to share my story. For that reason, I wrote down as much as I could during the experience. I wrote about the fear, the hopelessness, the depression, the hope (followed by more hopelessness), the rage, the disappointment each month, the longing, and the omnipresent impact that infertility was having on my life. I wanted to remember all the details so that if my dream of becoming a mother came true, I would more easily be empathetic to others struggling to attain motherhood.

I wanted to remember so that I would be able to feel gratitude each day for the kids I eventually did have, even with dark circles under my eyes, and while dealing with dirty diapers, tantrums, and whining.

In 2015, I announced my pregnancy with my first daughter on social media. I shared with a large group of friends and acquaintances that I had suffered two miscarriages and gone through two rounds of IVF before finally achieving a viable pregnancy.

Messages immediately began flooding my inbox from many women I hadn't heard from in years and some I wasn't close to, sharing that they, too, were struggling or had struggled to attain motherhood. I continued periodically to share details of my infertility journey on social media, and each time someone new contacted me looking for advice I gladly provided it to the best of my ability.

On Mother's Day 2019, I posted this message on social media:

> First, Happy Mother's Day to all the moms out there. You have an incredibly difficult job—really one of the hardest, and my mom friends inspire me almost daily. But we also have one of the most rewarding and fulfilling jobs and we moms are so blessed. Not only do I want to say Happy Mother's Day, but I also want to say in a very public way, to the women I know and even don't know well who might see this: if this day is a poignant reminder of a recent (or not so recent) loss, an estranged relationship, or a deep yearning with every fiber of your essence to be a mom—I am thinking of you and you are not forgotten on this day. You are amazing and strong and resilient.

In response, a good friend from high school urged me to write a book about my path to motherhood.

I had thought about such an endeavor before, but I told her I did not think my one story was enough to warrant an entire book. My friend suggested I include some "guest authors." I realized that there could be true strength in a collection of stories on this topic. So with her suggestion, this book was born.

From the beginning, I wanted to limit the stories in this book to those of women who experienced infertility and loss while on their path to motherhood and who ultimately were able to hold their baby—or babies—in their arms. This is because I felt that my purpose was to provide hope, and perhaps even help in some form, to those struggling with fertility concerns or pregnancy loss. I know some people may question my limiting the book to stories written by women, and specifically those who *have become* mothers to babies they hold in their arms. In no way do I consider the stories of women still on the path to motherhood and those of men who have struggled to attain fatherhood less important. I simply want to maintain a consistent focus.

I hope that the personal stories in this book not only provide hope to women struggling on their path to motherhood but also that the stories help foster a community of women who can offer advice, answer questions, and serve as a sounding board. My coauthors and I want to walk with you on your journey to motherhood, listen to your concerns, sympathize with what you're experiencing, and help ease your frustrations.

You may not choose to read every story in this book. I suggest reading the ones that call to you in some fashion.

Within each story, you may not relate to every experience or sentiment. That's OK.

Perhaps a particular story can provide the peace you need during your wait, making it more bearable.

Women walk different paths to motherhood. Mine was riddled with bumps and roadblocks. My story in this book serves as my memoir of the hardest path I have walked, but unquestionably the one with the sweetest reward at the end.

It is my sincere hope that my story and the stories of the eight other women in this anthology can offer you solace, hope, and a kindred connection while on your own path. I pray that some aspect of this book moves you closer—even in a small way—to that for which you yearn with every fiber of your essence: your baby in your arms, clarity, healing, or acceptance.

And if you feel so inclined, please indulge me by sharing a piece of your story with me. I would be forever grateful.

Godspeed, my friend.

Become part of our community by following us on Instagram @pathstomotherhood and visiting us at our website: **https://pathstomotherhood.wixsite.com/website**

The Bridge

KELLEY AUGSPURGER

I'm not here to tell you that everything is going to be OK.

The truth for me, and maybe for you as well, is that everything has changed. That all-consuming part of me, the core of who I am and my very essence, has been permanently altered. And the world around me? Nope. It keeps spinning without the slightest recognition that my heart has been ripped from my chest, leaving trails of negative pregnancy tests, an empty womb, and a crumpled-up shell of my former self.

At least that's what it feels like.

I need to tell you something about this feeling. (You need to lean in close because you might not be able to hear this right now.) This hole, this hurt, this time and space—it is so crushing and omnipresent *because it matters.* Your tears and your days when you cannot think of anything else—they matter. *You* matter. Your pain is part of your story and your journey. If you are in the midst of struggling with infertility, then right now feels like the most devastating part of your story, and it's certainly not the story you would choose. But you will go on and I believe you will be OK somehow. Just as that cruel world kept going each time another pee stick sent you to the floor in a heap of crushed hopes, tears, and despair, so too will your story. You are altered and scarred, but you will continue, one step at a time.

"How the hell do you know? You don't know that everything will be OK! No one can know that!" These are actual words I said to my husband when he tried to tell me everything would be OK.

How do I know life goes on? Well, science mostly. But here is my story, which I hope will help convince you at least a little.

"Mom"

In my younger days, I had no desire to be a mom. Not that I actively thought "Moms are stupid!" (Well, I probably did. I was a teenager.) I just did not have "Be a mother" on my life goals checklist. In my heart, I knew that one day I would want to adopt children. But the whole being pregnant, baby shower, mommy group thing? No, thank you. I had dreams of moving to the city, playing the guitar, and maybe singing in a subway to support myself until I made it big.

After I graduated from college and transitioned to adulthood, my standard of living became more acceptable to my mother, but the lifestyle I wanted still did not center on getting married and having children.

Imagine my surprise when I met the man I would marry in my early twenties.

I truly lucked out. Even before we were married, this man backed my every endeavor and encouraged me to continue to do the things I love, all while supporting me (not financially;

I make my own cheddar, ladies!). He didn't just put up with me, he loved the unpredictable and difficult traits that make me. So when the time came—and, believe me, I was just as surprised as everyone else that it did come—we decided to try for children the old-fashioned way.

Please indulge me while I say a few words about the old-fashioned way. It turns out my middle-school and high-school health classes were less than helpful in teaching me how my body actually works. Apparently, there is science behind reproduction: specific days, hormones, sperm counts. Who knew? Finding myself wanting children but woefully uneducated on conception, I did what any good millennial would do: Googled it and I talked to people on the internet about trying to get pregnant.

Have you ever told anyone you are trying to get pregnant? I don't recommend it. It doesn't matter who it is, their relation to you, or the length of your relationship. When you're in the Midwest and married without kids, everyone wants to talk to you about getting pregnant. Nay, not talk to you, share *all* their advice with you. Are you hoping to talk to that lady in the grocery store who you've never met about your "bedroom routines"? Head over to Middle America. These were some of my favorite gems (along with the responses I wish I'd given):

"Just relax! Stop trying so hard!" (Oh, that's the secret? Why didn't I think of that earlier?)

"Well, at least you get to enjoy trying!" (Timers and ovulation predictors—my idea of romance, for sure.)

"Being pregnant is the worst!" (I mean, maybe? I'd love to find out for myself.)

"Why not just adopt?" (Well, I can think of about 50,000 things standing between me and adoption—every one of them is dollars.)

"Think about all the travel and fun you can have without kids in the way!" (Totally. I'll give your kids away for you so that you can travel and have fun.)

"Everything happens for a reason."

I don't even have a snarky response for that last "piece of advice," which makes me shake and tense up just recalling it. Please, for the love of everything, never say that to anyone trying to get pregnant. If someone has said it to you, know that you have done nothing wrong. Every choice represents a plot point in your story, and your choices have made you who you are. I do understand that most people want to say something helpful and encouraging, but when your body fails to fulfill the most primitive responsibility in its female destiny, "Everything happens for a reason" can be devastating.

Medical Intervention

As you've probably guessed, the old-fashioned way did not yield the outcome for which I'd hoped. And so, after a year of trying, off to the doctor I went.

There are few things stranger than walking into a specialist's office as a seemingly healthy person. There are the feelings of guilt: with so much brokenness in the world, why do I have any right to complain? And there is also immense apprehension about what the doctors will or will not find. Walking into my specialist appointment for a consultation, I was flooded with emotions. My desire to find an answer was waning with every step I took in those sterile halls. Had it not been for the unshakeable presence of my husband, I don't think I would have been able to stay. Yet I went forward and proceeded with test after test.

After the hysterosalpingogram (HSG) to visualize my fallopian tubes, we heard "Don't worry! Most people end up getting pregnant after we clear out the tubes!" (We didn't.)

After multiple needles and a vast number of vials filled with my blood, our lab test results were in the normal range. This news was met with "That's a good sign! That means your body isn't preventing you from getting pregnant!" (It was.)

We were told that, if anything, my husband's "swimmers" were too strong. We heard, "There's a lot of them, so it's probably just hard for one to get through in the crowd." (Is that even a thing?)

After being prescribed the minimum dose of Clomid, we were told "Eight viable eggs! We are a little worried about multiples with all those available eggs, and you'll be pregnant in no time!" (We weren't.)

After round six of unsuccessful intrauterine insemination (IUI), we were finally confronted with the conclusion that "You have unexplained infertility."

Unexplained infertility means that medical professionals could not find a medical reason for why I was unable to get pregnant. Everything worked, and everything looked normal. Just unlucky, I guess.

To say I was devastated isn't exactly right.

Crushed? Yes.

Hopeless? Absolutely.

Numb? Completely.

As we grow up, we develop our core values: faith, commitment, optimism, good humor, education, courage, loyalty, patience, perseverance. When all is said and done, our values are the beliefs upon which we build our sense of self. We work hard to preserve them and prove that these beliefs are right, and our minds cling to them to provide a sense of order and control in a chaotic world. And when we find out that these core values we believed may not be true? Well, it can send a type-A control freak into an unexpected tailspin.

The day we received the unexplained infertility diagnosis, I walked out of the doctor's office with a lot of information. Yet I have no clear recollection of what was said. A very simple phrase, "We don't know what's wrong with you," shook me to my foundation. Two words, "unexplained fertility," created an intense doubt in all I had known to be true. My basic understanding of how the world works was forever changed. "How can my body just 'not work?' Wasn't I designed to do this? Why don't the experts know what is wrong?" I would spend the next months wrestling with these questions and my faith, trying to understand how I was going to cope with this new reality.

Mental Illness

Mental illness. Those are some bad words, huh? But do not stop reading. Mental illness does not always manifest in the form of a dramatic meltdown or even a visible disease. For some of us, it comes in like the first warm waters of a frozen river in spring. The ice that remains on top of the river gives the illusion that the river is still frozen and beautiful, but if you apply the slightest pressure, it all comes crashing down.

For me, depression was probably always underneath everything. And now that I know a few things about mental health, I can easily attribute many of my behaviors and reactions throughout my life to anxiety. Like many people, I characterized my depression as normal sadness resulting from a sad situation. Until one day, after we had been trying to get pregnant for more than a year and were in the midst of IUI treatments, I visited my gynecologist for my annual exam. I had tried to prepare myself mentally for the pregnancy question (I was married and smack dab in my prime childbearing years). When the nurse came in, one minute we were talking and laughing, and the next I was a bawling mess. She wisely summoned my doctor, who saw that I was not OK. She asked if I was seeing a therapist. When I said no, she handed me a referral to a psychiatrist.

I still thought I could handle the depression on my own. My breaking point, when I finally admitted that I needed help to get through my infertility journey, did not occur until six months later.

By that time, I had paused all fertility treatments. The drugs used for IUI were having a negative effect on my psyche, and the whole process was taking a toll on our marriage. The idea of putting new and much stronger drugs into my system made me physically ill. So, we decided to stop. It was an agonizing, painful, but ultimately necessary decision. I did my best to give myself grace. I successfully avoided baby showers and kids' birthday parties, which was beneficial in its own way. Yet missing out on social gatherings and the momentous events in my friends' lives was making me feel isolated.

Thanksgiving that year was seemingly normal: lots of people, ridiculous amounts of food, and drinks for days. And then came the Thanksgiving dinner pregnancy announcements.

Three in one day. There was nowhere for me to hide and no invitation to decline politely.

I felt like a stranger among the family whom I had grown to love. With each new announcement, followed by squeals of delight, I felt as if I was being sucker-punched in the gut, nearly rendering me breathless. I was embarrassed by my seemingly inappropriate reaction to this happiest of news. I also experienced crushing feelings of guilt because I assumed I was ruining the expectant mom's moment (I wasn't), and anger at myself for not feeling happy for her. After the third announcement, I could finally excuse myself. I sprinted to my car, laid the seat down flat so I could hide, and sobbed uncontrollably. I was miserable, and I was mad as hell, while at the same time all I wanted was to be inside celebrating and enjoying family time. I called my mother no less than four times that day sobbing uncontrollably. My mother picked up the phone each time and, as she had countless times throughout my infertility journey, listened to me vent. She didn't minimize my pain. Instead, she listened and gave me the space I needed to realize something was really wrong. After Thanksgiving, I got the help I desperately needed, which included a prescription for an antidepressant.

When it comes to prescription drugs, people typically have these questions: "What do they do to you? Are they a cure? Aren't they addictive? How do you keep from abusing them?" I'm not a doctor. I can only speak to my experience. For me, the antidepressant was not a miracle drug. It did not instantly make things better (and it certainly was not addictive—if anything, I wanted to go off of it as fast as I could). What it did do was give my brain and body a fighting chance at rebalancing the chemicals and hormones that were overwhelming my processing centers.

To be clear, I still had to put in the work. I had to allow myself the time and space to grieve the loss associated with being told I probably wouldn't be able to birth a child. I had to accept this reality and be kind to myself when I felt sad. I am glad I did put in the work; I'm a better person (and wife), and a more empathetic human for doing so.

The Light

One of the most incredible truths I have witnessed about humans is our perseverance and adaptability. When things do not go the way we hoped, planned, or intended, we are still capable of moving forward, pivoting, and recalibrating.

For my husband and me, the most meaningful pivot during our infertility journey was when we decided to pursue traditional adoption instead of moving forward with in vitro fertilization (IVF). The road to adoption is also a story riddled with disappointments, highs and lows, and crippling financial hurdles. And, for us, our road to adoption included steps forward and then backward (and then forward again): feeling mentally prepared and ready for the adoption process and then having moments in which we felt utterly overwhelmed and confused. The choice to adopt was easy; the emotions around waiting for your child were not. And it seemed that everywhere I looked there were stories I read in the news about women whose actions appeared objectively repugnant and incompatible with motherhood (but who had no problem getting pregnant), while I had to fight every day for the chance to give a child love and a good home. But fight for the chance to become parents is certainly what we did. We fought through mountains of paperwork. We fought to save enough money to afford adoption. We fought to prove to multiple state workers that we would provide a stable and safe home. We fought and waited and fought and waited.

Six months after starting the adoption process and a mere two-and-a-half weeks after becoming active candidates for adoption, all of our waiting (and fighting) came to a climax. One icy and snowy evening in 2013, we received a phone call that a baby boy had been born and his birth mother wanted us to be his parents. The most trying chapter of my life was finally coming to a close.

This time, two words again changed the course of my existence: "Congratulations, Mama."

Your Bridge

Infertility is a strange affliction to bounce back from. There is no typical grieving period, as you're not sure whether something was lost or if it never happened. Even when you know the cause of your infertility, there may be no obvious way to ensure conception and a healthy baby. And when you do finally attain the role of mother, the scars from the journey can remain raw and the trenches left behind from the fight for your baby can remain powerfully deep. Amidst all the changes in your life, you may wonder if it is possible to fully heal your wounded soul.

For many, the pain from these experiences never really goes away. In an attempt to escape from (or maybe just forget) the pain, you start to build a bridge over your river of grief. At first, it's no more than a few pieces of rope dangling over an abyss. A slip of your foot or a strong wind can send you hurtling back toward the bank. But after making it across a few times, you find ways to secure and strengthen your bridge. It becomes steadier and you fall off less frequently. Your baby, family, and friends become pillars and arches. You use your bridge to help others. At first, you may be ashamed to show it to others because it's just a rickety bridge, but in time, your bridge becomes more robust.

Eventually, you can't imagine life without it; it has become a landmark in your journey that others seek out for inspiration and hope. The river of pain below? It's still there. Maybe it always will be. As you accept that river as a part of what makes you beautiful and unique, though, it becomes a part of you instead of the whole of you.

Two children later, with the whole of life ahead of us (and much better than we imagined), I don't think I can go back to who I was before experiencing infertility; I don't think I can really "go back home." But why would I want to go back when what lies ahead is out there, just across the bridge, offering such promise and so much potential for transformation, rebirth, and a newfound and unconditional love? ■

KELLEY AUGSPURGER is a Missouri native who lives in the Kansas City area with her husband, two children, two cats, and two dogs. When not wrangling children, playing volleyball, or singing at local events, she manages the beverage program for the world's largest movie theatre company. In her free time, she co-founded a special events bakery business. You can follow Kelley on Instagram @charmingly__awkward.

The Road to an Only Child

MOLLY DEAN-CHANG

"You have a seven percent chance of conceiving a baby even with in vitro fertilization. Your lab results are similar to the results of a much older woman, and you don't ovulate normally."

Suddenly, I could not hear anything and the room became blurry as my heart broke into a million pieces. It had always been my dream to be a mommy, and this doctor was telling me that my chance of attaining that dream was only seven percent! My husband and I had been married less than a year, and now here I was, unable to give him a baby. I felt crushed, ashamed, embarrassed, and hopeless. These difficult feelings haunted me over the next two years during our infertility journey. This is the excruciating, yet ultimately beautiful, story of our path to becoming parents.

Beginning the Journey

I was 32 when I received the news of my grim chances of becoming a mother. I felt I didn't have a ton of time to wait around, so my husband and I chose to start fertility treatments right away.

However, after meeting with the stoic, cold, and statistic-centered doctor who had seemingly crushed my dream of becoming a mother, I decided that he was not the right fit for me. I needed a doctor who was warm and kind, and who exuded hope—not just someone who spouted numbers and statistics. I am a psychotherapist, after all, and appealing to my emotional side is crucial. (A piece of advice I now give other women going through infertility is to make sure you feel comfortable with your doctor and that he or she spends adequate time with you and provides you with some amount of hope.)

Fortunately, I quickly found a doctor who was a better fit. This new doctor suggested that we start with intrauterine insemination (IUI) and see how my body responded. I had no idea what this treatment entailed. I didn't know any other women who had gone through infertility, and I felt very alone, confused, overwhelmed, and isolated. I quickly ordered some fertility books, took to Google, and asked friends if they knew anyone who had gone through fertility treatments so I could contact them. I soon discovered that infertility is more common than I had initially thought, and I was connected with several women who talked to me about their experiences and gave me resources (and hope).

Some of these women suggested I try acupuncture to help increase my chances of success. More needles were par for the course! I went to acupuncture appointments one to two times per week and drank foul-smelling Chinese herbs for the next two years. Did it help? I have no idea, but it was a relaxing, albeit expensive, nap break.

Between seeing my reproductive endocrinologist and acupuncturist, I had a table full of at least 20 pill bottles, shots, herbs, and supplements. This alone was overwhelming. "Take this pill with food. Don't take this pill with food. Take this herb apart from any other medications. Take this supplement three times per day. This herb must be mixed with hot water, but taken only on an empty stomach." I had alarms going off all day (and even at night) to keep me on track. The routine was all-consuming. I felt like I had little space in my mind or time left for anything other than going to the numerous weekly appointments and managing my medication and herbal protocols. My anxiety, rooted in fear of the unknown, was sky-high. And the cocktail of fertility medications was not helping my anxiety level due to the hormonal changes associated with such medications.

Soon, I was in the middle of my first round of IUI. Sticking myself with needles was initially terrifying. The first time I stuck myself I fainted, but eventually it became a tired old routine. The medications and hormones made me extremely fatigued, left my brain feeling foggy, and I was moody at times. Bruises from the shots covered my stomach. I looked like someone had stomped all over me in high heels.

The IUI procedure itself did not take more than a minute. The two-week wait after the procedure was nerve-wracking as I waited for the call to find out if the IUI had worked. I got a call from the clinic telling me I had a positive pregnancy test result, but that it was a "low positive number." I had no idea what that meant. All I heard was "positive," and I was elated.

"Wow, this was not nearly as bad as I thought it would be. I can't believe I'm pregnant!" I thought. But, later that day, I got a call from the nurse, who explained that the low number most likely meant this was a chemical pregnancy that would result in a miscarriage, although there was still a possibility that it could "stick." I was devastated.

After this call, I had to pull myself together quickly to walk into a therapy session with my next client. I love what I do, but my personal infertility journey made it difficult at times to be present at work. And my infertility made it difficult at times to help patients sort through their issues because my own problems often felt so big and all-consuming. I even had some clients who vented to me about issues related to their children or deciding whether to have another child. This tore at my heart.

The phone call from the nurse was the beginning of the realization that this process would probably create an intensely difficult roller coaster of emotions.

Ultimately, the pregnancy resulted in my first miscarriage. To add insult to injury, our insurance did not cover a dime of our fertility treatments. Over the next two years we depleted our savings, borrowed money from our family, and ultimately spent about $100,000 to get our miracle baby. Talk about stressful! Who gets married and thinks that right away they will have to drop tens of thousands of dollars to create a baby? You are supposed to work on buying a home, traveling, and enjoying your marriage.

After the miscarriage, my husband and I were heartbroken. Some marriages break from the stress of infertility. I know people who ended up divorced shortly after going through fertility treatments. An infertility journey takes teamwork, compromise, communication, and a lot of understanding and patience.

Luckily, our marriage was strengthened by our fertility struggles, and I hope that because we got through this hardship, we can make it through whatever else the future holds.

Round Two

After my first pregnancy loss, the doctor recommended we try the IUI process again before moving on to something more invasive. She was hopeful that a second IUI would work because I had gotten pregnant the first time. However, the second round was another disappointment in that I didn't even get pregnant. We moved on to a third-round and endured yet another two-week wait. As anyone who has struggled with getting pregnant will tell you, those two weeks are excruciating! This time I got the call that I had another positive pregnancy test and the numbers were strong. I was thrilled, yet remained cautious in my optimism.

As the days went on, my human chorionic gonadotropin (hCG) levels increased as they were supposed to with a viable pregnancy. "Maybe this time it actually worked," I thought. I waited anxiously to go in for my first ultrasound, hoping to hear a heartbeat. I was extremely nervous about this appointment. Finally, the day of the appointment arrived. I still vividly recall waiting for the ultrasound technician to come into the exam room. I was lying on the exam table, in a dimly lit room, holding my husband's hand. Conflicting thoughts raced through my mind. I was sure we would hear a coveted heartbeat this time and I was already curious about the baby's gender. And then fearful thoughts would abruptly emerge, crushing those hopeful thoughts I had experienced a few moments before. After what seemed like an eternity, the ultrasound technician walked in, applied the cold gel, and inserted the ultrasound wand, allowing the moment of truth to reveal itself.

We did not see or hear a heartbeat. A flood of emotions swept over me: shame for hoping we would hear a heartbeat; disappointment that I had to seemingly stop mentally preparing for this baby; and anger that I apparently had to endure more waiting. The doctor came into the room and said nonchalantly, "Come back next week and hopefully we will see one. There is still hope!"

That next week was one of the most anxiety-ridden of my life. Finally, we went back and *still* no heartbeat. The doctor said, "It still could be hiding, so let's give it one more shot next week." I endured another week of hell, and then still no heartbeat. Apparently, I had a blighted ovum, which meant I had gotten pregnant, but the pregnancy never progressed and I was going to have another miscarriage. The doctor was concerned that it was an ectopic pregnancy. So many words I didn't understand, as I tried to process what the doctor was saying. I learned that if the pregnancy had been ectopic, I would have had to wait six to twelve months to try more treatments. Again, another devastation. I wanted a baby so badly that the thought of having to put the endeavor on hold for another year just about broke me.

Fortunately, the pregnancy was not ectopic. I went to the hospital for a dilation and curettage (D&C).

The Toll of Loss

The period of time after this miscarriage held some very dark days for me. I was so depressed that at times I did not know if I could go on. I felt like I was cursed or doomed or that the universe (or God) was punishing me. The plummeting of hormones after the miscarriage, coupled with the grief and sadness, at times felt too much to bear. Thanks to my husband and a couple of amazing friends and family members, I was able to get through this time and move forward.

Looking back on my infertility journey, I now know I was also experiencing a lot of anger. This was not fair! During my infertility journey, I would come to summon every skill I had ever learned (and taught) as a therapist to get through my journey and, in particular, my anger. My coping mechanisms throughout my journey were meditation, exercise, acceptance, letting go, surrendering, asking for help, self-care, and starting new hobbies to channel my energy. I tried knitting, gardening, painting—anything to distract my mind. These activities sometimes helped, but I still struggled immensely nearly every day. There was a great deal of crying and breaking down to my husband due to the stress, heartbreak, anxiety, and hormones. And during my fertility treatments, my medical team discouraged the use of many of my usual lifelines: exercise, hot yoga, warm baths, and wine. I was on a strict diet as well, so cooking the recommended organic and unprocessed foods was also time-consuming and stressful.

Another important part of my making it through infertility was therapy. Even so, I struggled to find a therapist who truly understood what I was going through and was educated about the infertility process. There didn't seem to be a plethora of therapists who were truly knowledgeable about infertility. This is partly why I am now passionate about making my therapy practice especially welcoming to, and appropriate for, infertility patients.

Beginning IVF

When the prior pregnancy had not turned out to be an ectopic pregnancy, we were thankful to be able to try again. The doctor recommended that we try one final IUI after I healed from the D&C and before exploring in vitro fertilization (IVF). We did, and it was again unsuccessful. Around this time I found out that I likely had what is called "poor egg quality" and that this was probably why I was having unsuccessful pregnancies.

Now it was time to bring out the big guns and try IVF. My body was covered in bruises, I had gained 20 pounds, I had acne from the hormones, my mood was unpredictable, and I felt like a shell of my former self. IVF meant more shots, more pills, stronger hormones, more time-intensive regimens and appointments, and of course, more money. I felt we had no choice. Either we moved forward with this horrible process or I might never get to be a mommy to a child who was genetically tied to my husband and me. Along the way, people would make comments such as, "Why don't you just adopt?" or "Lots of people have happy lives without kids." Adoption is a blessing and the people who adopt children are angels on Earth. Adoption was not out of the question for us, but I really wanted to experience pregnancy, if possible.

I should also add that the question "Why don't you just adopt?" is never something helpful to say to someone going through infertility. In fact, I ended up losing friendships through this process, as some people were not capable of being supportive, understanding, or empathetic. I had no room for those kinds of people in my life. Yet losing those friendships was difficult and added to the grief I was already experiencing. I can now see that discovering who my true friends were, and learning what makes a meaningful friendship endure, was fortuitous.

We moved on to IVF. Our first round was another disappointment. I had read in online forums about women having 20, 30, or 40 eggs retrieved at one time. I got only eight! The doctor tried to comfort me by saying that the number of eggs was less important than the quality of eggs. Because I had already had two miscarriages, we tested my embryos for chromosomal abnormalities ("PGS testing"). After a couple more weeks of anxiously waiting to see how the embryos developed, we ended up getting only one chromosomally normal embryo.

Again, I was devastated. After all the money, hormones, and physical and emotional pain, we only got one embryo? I was livid. I had been set on having two children, and now even one child seemed out of the question. My husband encouraged me to take a break from the physical and emotional stress of IVF, but I couldn't do it. I am a type-A person. I had a goal; I wanted to achieve it, and I wanted to do so *now.*

We moved forward with another round of IVF medications and another egg retrieval, hoping for more healthy embryos before undergoing a transfer.

This time the doctor put me on the maximum possible dosage of hormones because apparently, I was a "poor responder" to medications. This IVF round resulted in the same outcome: eight eggs. We played the waiting game again and ended up with two healthy embryos. OK, I thought, I can work with a total of three. Three embryos could get me the two babies I dreamt of. I felt hopeful, but also terrified. "What if it doesn't work? What if we go through all of this and spend all this money and still don't get a baby?" I even started researching adoption as a backup plan to ease my mind. My mantra became, "You will be a mommy one day; somehow or some way." This helped me when I went to the dark and hopeless places in my mind.

Now it was time to prepare my uterus for an embryo transfer. We decided to implant two of the three embryos because we were comfortable with the possibility of having twins. The physical preparation for the transfer included more procedures to get my body and uterus in tip-top shape and some of them were painful. Then we had to make more decisions about what "add-ons" we wanted. There are things like "embryo glue" and "intra-lipid IV treatments" that you can try that might increase the chances of a successful pregnancy. I have to wonder if some of these extras may not necessarily be helpful and instead are merely a way for doctors to obtain more money. Because you're so scared you're willing to do and pay anything to increase your chances. We said "yes" to it all. I never wanted to doubt myself and wonder "Well, if I had done XYZ, maybe that would have made it work." So, to ease my anxiety, we dropped even more money on all the extras. Money felt like Monopoly money to me by that point and I was numb to the spending. On the bright side, we had more airline miles than we could count—we later essentially got a "free" babymoon thanks to credit card points.

Finally, after two very long and arduous years of infertility, the big day was here. The day of our embryo transfer was probably one of the scariest of my life. I tried to be optimistic, but I was petrified. So much seemed to be at stake. Throughout our infertility journey, my husband was always the grounding and optimistic force that kept me going, and he appeared to be sure it would work. I tried to harness some of his energy as I walked into the room for the transfer. The doctor showed me images of the two embryos, then quickly inserted them. And that was that. All that hype and adrenaline for a 30-second procedure. It was surreal. I was "pregnant until proven otherwise."

The Joy of Success

Now for another dreaded two-week wait to determine if I was pregnant. This one was even more excruciating than the previous waits. The doctors and nurses advised against doing at-home pregnancy tests before the official blood test at the office. I did not listen. Eight days after my transfer, I took a home pregnancy test. I did not tell my husband what I was doing because I knew he would tell me not to take the test. I walked into the bathroom to pee on the stick and my hand was shaking so hard that it was tricky to do the test. I felt like I was going to pass out and throw up. I held my breath and waited in angst. To my great surprise, there was a plus sign! And it was a pretty dark line (a good indicator). I went to wake my husband up and said, "It worked! I am pregnant!"

We were still extremely wary, not wanting to get our hopes up; my husband did not even seem excited, as I think he was trying to protect his heart and mine. At this stage, it seemed dangerous to get too excited or attached to the idea of a baby.

A couple of days later, the blood test confirmed the pregnancy and my numbers rose steadily. In fact, my hCG numbers were so high that the doctor mentioned it was possible I could be pregnant with twins. Still, I experienced so much anxiety. What if we went to the ultrasound and there was no heartbeat again? What if I had another miscarriage? I did not think my mind or body could withstand another miscarriage.

At the first ultrasound appointment, we heard the sweet sound we had been waiting so very long to hear. Finally, we felt joy and amazement hearing the utterly beautiful and bold sound of a heart beating. We also felt immense relief. Yet we were still cautious and scared. As the weeks went on, the baby grew bigger and appeared healthy.

At ten weeks we "graduated" from the fertility clinic and I was able to see a regular OBGYN. I had a couple of complications along the way, but everything turned out OK.

Several months later, I gave birth to our perfect and healthy baby girl. Her birthday was the most amazing day of our lives. She is the center of our universe and brings us joy every single day. Our daughter is so loved, and she will one day know how much we wanted her and how hard we worked to bring her here.

When our daughter was two, we decided we should try to implant our remaining embryo. My husband and I felt torn about this decision. We were so happy with our family of three that we were no longer sure we wanted another child. Nor were we sure we wanted to put my body through the agony of the shots, pills, and hormones again. And there was the potential of enduring another miscarriage. Some women do not have many negative side effects from the shots and medications, but my body was extremely sensitive. Nonetheless, we decided we at least should try.

After only a couple of weeks on the fertility medications, I was not doing well. I think my body was beat up and had become even more sensitive to the hormones. I was unable to think straight or function normally. I became very depressed and even started having suicidal thoughts. And I was exhausted. I felt like a zombie. I could barely take care of our daughter and myself. Ultimately, we decided that my physical and mental health were more important than a second child, so we decided to stop the process and go back to enjoying our family of three.

While I had always wanted two children, I quickly found acceptance around having just one child. This acceptance stemmed partly from the clarity that trying for a second child was not worth wrecking my physical and emotional health and partly from the contentment and happiness we experienced with having just one child. I'd like to believe that my infertility journey contributed to our deep gratitude for, and contentment with, our family of three.

Gratitude and Growth

I am thankful for what we went through and all those dark days because, without them, we would not have our perfect daughter.

What did I learn from my infertility journey? Upon reflection, I believe my infertility journey taught me how to be more patient. Being patient undoubtedly makes me a better parent. I learned that I married the right man; he is the most amazing father. I learned that I have no space in my life for people who are not genuine and supportive. I learned that I strongly value—and want to protect—my precious time with my husband and daughter. And most importantly, I learned I am stronger than I initially thought.

After enduring infertility and recurrent pregnancy loss, I felt compelled to help other women and men going through this dark and lonely journey. As a psychotherapist, I now regularly counsel those struggling through infertility and experiencing postpartum depression or anxiety, and those who have experienced traumatic births. I can only hope that my experience, perspective, and advice can help ease some other people's pain and provide them with hope. ■

MOLLY DEAN-CHANG lives in Phoenix, Arizona with her husband and daughter. Both she and her husband are Phoenician natives. Molly works as a psychotherapist in private practice. She specializes in working with trauma and PSTD, depression (including postpartum), anxiety, disordered eating, and infertility and pregnancy loss. Molly loves hiking, reading, exploring nature, traveling, hot yoga, and spending time with her family and friends. You can contact Molly directly through her website at www.AnewpathAZ.com

From Terror to Triumph

JANELLE A. DIXON

I grew up in a strict Christian home where sex before marriage was frowned upon. While I'm sure those who spoke on the subject encouraged us to "save ourselves" for spiritual reasons, the reason I most frequently heard cited was to avoid pregnancy. Premarital sex was so openly and vehemently denounced that I can honestly say I was afraid of getting pregnant before I even started having sex. For as long as I can remember, church and the teachings that came along with it, were the epicenter of my life. When I was not at school, I was at church. Church was so synonymous with who I was that my school classmates nicknamed me "Church Girl." My family and I attended church five out of seven days a week. On Monday, my siblings and I sat in the pews in the back while my mother attended church business meetings; Tuesday was for youth ministry meetings; Wednesday meant mandatory evening Bible study; We spent Thursday in choir rehearsal; and on Sunday, we spent the entire day at church, beginning with Sunday school and ending with an evening service. Church was our home away from home. We wore our Sunday best in and out of the sanctuary; girls were not allowed to wear pants until shortly before I celebrated my first double-digit birthday (this was the 1990s!). I made my first friends at church. My value system was developed within the church walls, and I believed the teachings shared in church were the most important lessons I would ever learn.

Many of the adults at my church served as surrogate family members, and they created the roadmap for the kids' lives. The expected trajectory could be summed up by "First comes love, then comes marriage, then comes a baby in a baby carriage." But as teenage pregnancies began to show up, my peers and I were confronted with different realities and examples of what life could look like. And as relatives and close family friends became unwed teenage mothers and fathers, the adults closest to me began to drill a more explicit message into my head: "No sex before marriage or else!"

With teenage pregnancy such a hot-button issue, I spent most of my adolescent years preoccupied with the thought of sex leading to pregnancy. I began to fantasize that, like Mary, I would become pregnant without ever having sex, but worried that my mother, unlike Joseph, would never believe me when I told her that *This was all Jesus's doing.* So, I ignored the notes that boys passed me in the hallway and kept my distance from them at school dances. I was determined to be the good girl my parents and church family wanted (and expected).

Motherhood, Here I Come

That all changed when I left for college and met a man. After experiencing my first taste of freedom and autonomy, I fell hard. Soon enough the relationship progressed beyond mere kissing and holding hands and, well, it did so *sans* birth control. From that relationship, my first daughter was born.

My daughter was the miracle I had been blessed with, and I set out to ensure that she never went without. As my romance with her father quickly fizzled, I found myself a 19-year-old unwed mother. This label motivated me to prove to my family that I really could do it all. I spent the next several years proving that I could parent adeptly, finish college, and maintain a social life, even if doing it all might cost me my identity and freedom. I focused intently on the success that I hoped would mitigate the sex I had had before marriage.

When my daughter was born, I knew she depended on me, and that there wasn't anything I wouldn't do for her. I nursed her while I studied, scheduled classes around her nap times, attended classes with her on my hip, and graduated from college with her by my side.

However, I was so focused on proving to those around me that a teenage pregnancy didn't mean my life was over that I didn't allow myself the time or space to marvel at the creation of life. Surrogate family members had spent many years attempting to dissuade me from having sex so I wouldn't get pregnant, but when I finally did, I was unprepared to appreciate the beauty that *is* pregnancy. The adults in my life had failed to talk to me about all the tiny miracles that must happen to create a child. I had become convinced that getting pregnant was so easy that I took for granted the wonders happening inside my body. I never once thought it might be difficult to conceive or birth a child. I *expected* my daughter's arrival and counted on it as if I were entitled to it. Instead of counting myself blessed to be pregnant, I spent my pregnancy counting down the days until her appearance and planning the life I wanted to give her. I was on a mission to curate a life I'd been taught I could attain during all those hours at church. After her birth, I set out on that mission. My daughter propelled me toward my dreams, and with her by my side, I completed my undergraduate degree, attended law school, and made significant strides in my professional career.

Then I met the man with whom I would spend the rest of my life and began to dream about my "happily ever after." When it was time to settle down and do pregnancy the "right way," I was ecstatic about the thought of creating life with my beloved husband. I daydreamed about the opportunity to share the responsibility of child-rearing with someone who shared my values and whom my family adored.

A Second Pregnancy

After our wedding, it didn't take long before we were growing from a family of three into a family of four. Corey and I were married in March and I was pregnant by May. As a first-time parent, Corey was overjoyed. Watching him beam with pride, knowing that I'd played a role in creating his smile, was life-changing.

With excitement and anticipation, we began to tell those closest to us about our pregnancy. I told my parents and close friends about the bundle of joy who would be joining us. And I recall the excitement in their voices when they told me how happy they were for me. My closest cousin and I hadn't gotten 10 minutes into a phone call before she started planning my baby shower. I knew this new baby would be loved and welcomed.

But as I sat in my office just weeks after sharing the news, drafting whatever legal document had been asked of me, I began to feel a tugging. I ignored it.

Later in the day, my stomach began to cramp, and when the cramping became more uncomfortable than I could stand, I excused myself to go to the restroom. Sitting alone in the restroom stall, I saw the blood. I sat there for what felt like an eternity, completely perplexed. My mind raced back to the calls we'd made that prior weekend. I padded my underwear with tissue and raced back to my office without making eye contact with anyone in the hallway. When I Googled "bleeding during pregnancy," I found information about minimal implantation bleeding, which I hoped would calm my fears. Yet deep down I knew that the blood was more than a little spotting.

I left work early. On my way home, I called my husband and I told him about the blood. He assured me in the best way he knew how that all was well. Still, I worried. As I sat on the train during the hour-long commute from the city to the Chicago suburbs, I vacillated between tears and stoicism. As I watched the cityscape turn from high rises to tree-lined neighborhoods, I wondered if I would soon be pushing a stroller down a similar street, or if my fantasy was rapidly fading. I knew what this was: I was failing. *But why? Why now?*

At home, I waited for my husband. By the time he arrived, I'd soaked through the wadded-up tissue, but I refused to use a sanitary napkin for fear of the message I'd be sending myself. In my mind, a pad would make it real. The Christian in me was holding fast to the faith I'd been taught to cling to in times of trouble. I padded my underwear a second time.

My husband and I ultimately decided that it would be a good idea to go to the emergency room. We had no babysitter for my 10-year-old daughter, so she accompanied us. There, in hushed whispers, I told the nurses what was going on, and we waited. They brought me into the room, drew my blood, asked a lot of questions, and then the nurses were off to run tests. The sterile hospital was cold and eerily quiet but for the sounds of beeping machines and staff completing their rotations. I sat on the white sheets, afraid to stand up out of fear that I'd see blood beneath me. As we sat in the quiet room watching the nightly news, the on-call doctor joined us. She complimented me on my hair and asked how I was feeling. I looked into her eyes as she went over my medical history, searching for the answer I wanted. I began to grow impatient. Looking back, I realize she was trying to cushion the bad news. In a hushed tone, she told me that based on my calculations as to how far along the pregnancy was, my hormone levels did not match what was expected. She confirmed my greatest fear: I was losing my baby.

I let out a horrible wail—a sound unlike anything I'd heard myself make. It was the sound of anguish, the sound of failure, the sound of disbelief that my body was not doing what it was meant to do. My daughter, who had been sleeping, woke up to my crying and asked, "Is something wrong with the baby, Mommy?" "Did the baby die?" The answer was too heavy for me to carry. I'd spent my entire life thinking it was easy to get pregnant and trying to avoid it. I was unprepared for the weight of this loss. I pulled myself together and I did what I thought I needed to do: lied to her. I told her there had never been a baby; that I was only sad because I had been mistaken. And with that lie, I buried my baby.

While I waited to be discharged, I watched my daughter sleep. I sat thinking about how silly I'd been to take her entrance into the world for granted. Tears stained my face as

I watched my husband, who'd once beamed with pride, try his hardest to hold it together for me. He rubbed my back, paced the room, and plugged away on his phone.

That night, I didn't sleep. I held my stomach, hoping that the emergency room doctor had gotten it wrong. She hadn't.

Adding Insult to Injury

"You should try to catch it."

Those had been my doctor's orders after my emergency room visit. "And if you catch it over the weekend, be sure to freeze it. I'd like to take a look at it to make sure all the tissue has been expelled."

I'll never forget those words, and those instructions raced through my head as my daughter and I walked back from Baskin-Robbins and I felt "it." The surrounding traffic seemed to slow down, and I struggled to visualize the crosswalk sign. The doctor told me it would feel like a rush of fluid, and it did. She told me I'd know it when it happened, and I did. "You shouldn't feel much pain," she'd said, "The worst is over." But I did feel pain, and the worst wasn't over.

I slowed down as we walked, trying to hold my legs together. I asked my daughter to tell me a story. I was not about to ruin this day for her. After all, this was the first time in days that I'd had any desire to leave the house. I walked slowly and kept a smile on my face as she rode her bike beside me and shared her story.

When we made it home, I grabbed a Tupperware container that I'd received as a wedding gift a few months earlier, and, again, excused myself to the bathroom. There, I caught it.

Or him.

Or her.

I sat in the bathroom for what felt like an eternity. I sat holding my baby in a Tupperware container. And because I'd caught my baby on a Saturday, it had to spend the weekend in the freezer alone.

I avoided the kitchen that weekend, ordering out instead. I hated the thought of what I'd had to do. The freezer reminded me of what felt like a failure; that I wasn't able to do something that for years I'd thought was so easy. I felt like I'd let my excited family down: my husband, who couldn't stop talking about the joy he felt knowing he'd be a dad; my daughter, whom I'd lied to; my baby and myself.

The feeling of failure never quite went away. And having failed to give myself time to properly grieve the loss of my child, I did not truly explore what was informing those feelings at the time. Instead, despite my hesitations, I agreed to give pregnancy another try.

It wasn't until that point that I began to realize the cosmic size of my grief.

Grief for me was, and continues to be, very tricky. It continues to show up when I least expect it and in the most unpredictable ways. My grief created anxiety and worry in all the wrong places and at all the wrong times. So, when I was pregnant with my second daughter a year later, in addition to carrying her for nine months, I carried the weight of worry from my past "failure." Feelings of failure followed me into every doctor's appointment. Those feelings made me question myself and my body's capabilities throughout each trimester. Feelings of failure and unresolved grief resulted in my being admitted to Labor and Delivery at least three times before giving birth because I was so worried that she was trying to come early. At every turn, my doctor's *inaccurate* words echoed in my ear, "You shouldn't feel much pain. The worst is over." Despite her attempt to reassure me, I did feel pain. In fact, I still feel it, and the loss of my child has never really felt "over."

Embracing Loss and Harnessing Strength

It has taken quite a while to shake the survivor's remorse I've felt since losing my child. While it would be easy to find solace in the old saying "Time heals all wounds," that has not been my experience. Although I am no longer bleeding, I continue to feel the pain from the wound that is the loss of my child. I don't expect that this grief will ever really be over, even if it gets easier to manage.

Recently, after giving birth to a third daughter, I gave myself permission to say I was finished having children. Although I had been feeling this way for quite some time, I hesitated to say it out loud. I knew many women wished they had the opportunity to have a child and so I felt guilty for the privilege of being able to choose to not have any more children. Yet, voicing my desire to not have more children has been integral to managing my grief, tending to my wound, and remembering my loss.

Owning my pain and embracing my loss has given me strength I never knew I possessed. It has allowed me to speak with women about miscarriage, and I have stood in the gap with women who believed they were alone in their struggles. My friends, who know I've experienced a miscarriage, reach out to me when someone close to them goes through something similar. They seek my advice on how they can be there for that friend or family member, and I happily talk with them about what helped me through the experience and what has given me strength. No longer do I feel like a failure because I am confident I did not fail. Instead, the terror I experienced has slowly transformed into triumph. The loss that I experienced has allowed me to be a greater asset to my children. The miscarriage I endured has sharpened my empathy and gifted me another layer of love to share with those who need it most.

When the time is right for me to start discussing sex and pregnancy with my three daughters, I plan to share my stories of struggle as well as triumph. I hope they will never feel alone as they embark on their own paths to motherhood. I will be transparent with them about the fragility of pregnancy and all of its wonder. I will correct the lie I told my first daughter in the hospital room years ago. I will assure my daughters that the only "right way" to get pregnant is to identify what looks and feels right to them. They will grow up learning about the miracle of pregnancy, they will learn about the tenderness of sex within a loving relationship, and I will encourage them to feel empowered to make decisions that are right for them. I hope they will grow to understand that our paths in life are not always the paths we envision traveling.

I am confident that without experiencing my own pregnancy loss, I would not have thought to emphasize these important points to my daughters. My path to motherhood, and in particular, my miscarriage, has undoubtedly influenced the dialogues I have started with my daughters, and it will continue to influence the conversations we have in the future. I'd like to think I will be able to gently guide my daughters down their own paths to motherhood in an empathetic, compassionate, and open-minded manner. And I'd like to think this story might help guide you, in some way, down your own path as well. ■

JANELLE DIXON lives with her husband and three daughters in Elgin, Illinois. Janelle is a litigator, whose professional focus is primarily on the representation of community associations. In 2020, she became the first African-American partner in her firm's 36-year history. Janelle enjoys volunteering in her community, coaching the Chicago-Kent's trial team, and teaching Sunday School in her spare time. You can contact Janelle at Janelle.Fairchild@yahoo.com.

Winding Road to Motherhood

SUSAN SWEETLAND GARAY

Longing is a story.

A large enough story to fill pages and time. We write what we long for. Families. Love. Babies. Time for ourselves. Safety. Community. To be known and seen and truly heard. To save the planet. To save the children who cannot save themselves.

We plant all the seeds and see what comes up.

I planted 1,000 seeds that I'd been given at a friend's funeral, which had been sitting in a dark kitchen drawer for years. I thought only a precious few of them would bloom, but the pot was soon overflowing with green seedlings reaching up, higher and further than I imagined they could; ready to be given away and planted.

My infertility story has felt a little like that. Desperate and without hope at times, yet overflowing with life at others.

Infertility and pregnancy loss are traumatic. Those who have not been through it wildly underestimate this trauma. But if we have, we just keep planting seeds and waiting to see what comes up.

Those of us in this community—this community of women who experience challenges getting and staying pregnant—seem usually to have at least one common characteristic. Specifically, many of us are eternal optimists.

My story does have a happy ending. A messy, confusing, chaotic, happy ending. But not every story has one, and I know I am one of the lucky.

I have two beautiful children and we are contemplating trying for a third. Neither of my children would exist without science and medical intervention. If I had been born a number of years earlier, I would not have been able to have children.

Discovering the Issue

My primary issue with getting pregnant was, and continues to be, endometriosis. Endometriosis affected my egg quality and the ability of fertilized eggs to implant in my uterus. I got married in 2012 knowing from my experience in a previous marriage that I would have trouble getting pregnant, but no one had identified my specific problem.

Knowing my husband and I would likely experience issues, and because I was already 32, we started trying to conceive soon after we got married. No surprise: I did not get pregnant. So, we made an appointment at a local hospital that had a fertility clinic. We underwent some tests, and the medical team suggested we first try intrauterine insemination (IUI).

The procedure was unsuccessful. In addition, during all the ultrasounds I had leading up to it, they found a large cyst on one of my ovaries.

Finding that cyst was reason enough to go in for an exploratory laparoscopy. The surgery was minimally invasive, and it seemed to be our best move toward trying to find answers.

My OBGYN, who was a fine enough surgeon—though not a specialist, and she didn't fully understand (or care) that our primary goal was fertility—performed the surgery. I also did not fully understand what was at stake or that I couldn't always completely trust that a doctor was doing what was best for my unique body. So, I listened to what I was told instead of doing my own research.

The surgery went well. The doctor performed an ablation to cauterize quite a bit of endometriosis, and she removed most of one ovary. Excision is generally a better method for removing endometriosis, but I was not aware of this at the time of the ablation.

When I woke up, I was delighted to have an endometriosis diagnosis. The relief of finally having an answer was incredible. I just hoped that knowledge would translate into a treatment plan that would bring me a baby.

It turned out that we would not have to wait long. In the first month after my surgery, we were allowed to try to conceive. I got pregnant. I had no idea how extremely rare and unusual this was, and how lucky we were that it worked out that way.

The pregnancy was easy, and I was blissfully unaware of all the things that could have gone wrong.

I went into labor three weeks early and gave birth to a baby girl. She weighed about five and a half pounds but was perfectly healthy and not considered premature.

After she was born, we found out I had a small placenta and a weak umbilical cord, and that my body probably would not have been able to support her if the pregnancy had gone to term. We were fortunate we got to walk away with our beautiful baby girl.

Second Opinions

When my daughter was two, we started thinking about trying for another baby. We had hoped that my being pregnant and then nursing would keep the endometriosis at bay long enough that we could again get pregnant naturally. However, when I was completely finished breastfeeding and still not pregnant, we began to think we needed a little more medical intervention. Surgery had worked well before, so it seemed like a good place to start.

I met with the same doctor who had performed the surgery the first time. She thought it was a good idea to do it again. And when I asked about the possible side effects and risks to my overall fertility, she said there was nothing to be worried about.

Around this time, my husband had started a new job. He worked for a small vineyard management company in the Willamette Valley, farming small, privately owned properties. One of the vineyards happened to be owned by a semiretired reproductive endocrinologist who had a very well-respected clinic in Portland, Oregon.

One day, just weeks before I was supposed to have my second surgery for endometriosis, my husband decided he felt comfortable enough with this vineyard owner to tell him about our situation and ask his opinion. After hearing our story, the doctor told him that under no circumstances should I have the surgery. Full stop.

We were shocked. This highly regarded man clearly knew what he was talking about. Our surgeon did not. She had told us that there were no risks to my fertility worth mentioning. This specialist told us that each time a surgeon touches your ovaries, damage is done. Eggs are lost. And for a woman in her thirties (I was 37), who may or may not have had many eggs left to work with, that was a big deal.

He advised that, at the very least, before we moved forward, we talk to one of the excellent doctors at his clinic. He made a call, and they got us in within a week.

I liked the reproductive endocrinologist I saw right away. She was personable and caring and clearly knew what she was talking about. She seconded what the other doctor had said: surgery was a good idea if the goal was to get rid of the pain associated with endometriosis, but probably not if the goal was to have a baby. I had already lost most of one ovary in the first surgery. I did not, of course, have unlimited eggs, and the ones I did have had probably been damaged by the endometriosis. If we wanted another baby, this doctor's recommendation was in vitro fertilization (IVF).

I am aware that the diagnosis a doctor gives, and his or her recommended treatment, may likely derive from his or her specialty. For example, if a doctor specializes in cancer, he or she is probably more likely to look for and think that signs are pointing to cancer. But I felt strongly that we had been led to the option of IVF. My husband happened to have a new job in which he had the ear of a well-regarded reproductive endocrinologist, who happened to have a clinic that he could pull strings to get us into—and all of that happened just weeks before we had planned for me to have a second surgery. It all seemed too perfect to be a coincidence.

So, we jumped into IVF.

It was a world full of appointments and medications and detailed instructions. I felt great because we were actually doing something. I finally had a long, extensive list of things I could do to try to get what I wanted (another baby). It was also such a relief to have tasks I could check off of my list that would bring me closer to a baby. And I was pretty good at it managing the task of IVF. I am organized when I need to be, and it basically felt like an enormous project that I could manage. I was diligent. I bought a giant pill box for all my supplements and medications so that I would remember what to take when. I perfected the art of giving myself shots in the stomach.

This is not to say the IVF process was easy. On the contrary, the process was undoubtedly taxing and time-consuming.

I knew that we were not guaranteed a baby at the end of the IVF process, but I believed we would be successful.

When my egg follicles were large enough and we had as many as were reasonable to hope for (with my having only one and an eighth working ovaries, plus low ovarian reserve), I went in for the egg retrieval.

The doctor was able to retrieve eight eggs. That was not a fabulous number. Some women end up with 20 or more, but eight was pretty good given all my issues. We then had to wait to see how many eggs were mature and how many of them were fertilized by my husband's sperm. By day three we had five embryos still growing.

With each passing day, you expect some embryos' growth to start to slow. We were just hoping that in the end, we would have an embryo to transfer. We knew it only takes one good embryo, but this waiting phase to find out how many (if any) viable embryos you still have was hard.

Typically, a doctor allows an embryo to grow for five days in a lab before transferring it to the uterus. On the morning of my transfer, the lab technician called to tell me that we had two embryos still growing well and one that might keep growing. The plan was to do a "fresh transfer" (as opposed to a frozen one) of the two best embryos and then freeze and genetically test any extras to use in the future if necessary.

When we arrived at the appointment, we found out that the third embryo had stopped growing. This was disappointing, but we still had two embryos to transfer.

The transfer process was easy; I was fully awake for the whole thing. Afterward, I had two days of bed rest before returning to work and normal life. Then I waited about 10 days before taking a blood pregnancy test.

I was anxious on the day of the pregnancy test. I got up early, drove to Portland, and waited for the clinic to call with the results. I finally called the clinic and was told that the test was positive, but that the human chorionic gonadotropin (hCG) number—the number that indicates the amount of pregnancy hormone in your blood—wasn't great. However, the number was high enough that the nurses all said congratulations and not to worry.

I would go back in for another test two days later. I was still anxious but tried to relax and enjoy the positive pregnancy test result. Some well-meaning co-workers even got me balloons, which I happily accepted. I felt like it was a time to celebrate, and I did not want to end up feeling like I had missed out on this early happy period of pregnancy because of my anxiety.

With the next blood test, the clinic wanted the hCG number to have doubled. My number had, so I could relax a bit. Throughout this whole process, I was nervous but confident.

I still felt that some caring force in the universe had led us to IVF and that we would, therefore, be successful. I heard all the time about women with very low hCG numbers who went on to give birth to healthy babies. I just figured I would be one of those women.

About two weeks after the first blood test, my husband and I went in for the first ultrasound. It went well; the doctor could see all the things she was supposed to see, and we heard a strong heartbeat. We both felt relieved and elated. At the end of the ultrasound, the doctor said she didn't want to cause unnecessary worry, but that the baby was a little small. It was possible the baby would catch up in growth or that the egg had implanted later than expected.

We were a little concerned but mostly we felt good about the heart rate and hopeful that things would look better in a week, at the next ultrasound. I went to the next two appointments alone. Both times the baby was still small but had a strong heartbeat and was continuing to grow. It seemed more and more like we just had to have faith and keep waiting patiently and things would turn out all right.

At my next appointment when I was 10 weeks pregnant, the Friday before Thanksgiving, I had decided that I was going to stop worrying and enjoy being pregnant. Being anxious wasn't good for the baby or me, and I needed to relax and enjoy how far I'd come.

On the way to the appointment, I took myself out for a solo lunch. In the waiting room, I smiled at strangers. I finally was not so afraid.

After a blood draw, I had my ultrasound.

It all happened fast after that. It took the reproductive endocrinologist only a second or two of glancing at the screen to determine that I had lost the baby. "There's no heartbeat," she said as she removed the ultrasound wand. I had not had time to study the screen; I wondered, "Maybe the heartbeat is just hard to find? Maybe we are not looking hard enough?"

I do not remember much of what was said after that. The doctor asked if I had questions. I stared at her blankly. I would have questions, many questions, but not at that moment. She told me to visit my OBGYN to talk about the next steps. She said she was so sorry.

Then she was gone, and I was mechanically getting dressed. I opened the door, and the nurse was waiting for me. A fertility clinic does not want a shocked and heartbroken woman walking through its waiting room, upsetting the hopeful patients there. She led me to a back way out of the office.

I called my husband and finally started to cry. I was so shocked and numb that I had not felt much of anything. It just felt unreal.

I had to drive an hour to get home. The rest of the day was a blur. I texted work that I wasn't coming in and asked my mom to pick up my daughter from school. I did not call my sister until the next morning. I then told my parents and in-laws that we had lost the baby.

On a whim, my husband and I decided that we wanted to go to the coast that weekend. We wanted to bring all of our family together and circle the wagons. So, the next morning, my husband, our daughter, and I, as well as my parents, sister, and in-laws, all went to the family beach house to be together and try to be soothed by the ocean's waves.

The weather wasn't great, and I hardly left the house. Everyone took care of my daughter and I was left alone to live in the quiet, sad space in my head as I tried to comprehend my new reality.

On Saturday evening, my husband and I walked to a small cliff overlooking the ocean, where we saw the most glorious and colorful sunset I've ever seen on the Oregon coast. There were shades of orange, pink, yellow, and purple. Those colors, reflected in the water, creating a silhouette of the rocks and pine trees, felt like a gift. A gift from the universe or from our baby, whose heart had stopped beating.

Being Present Through the Pain

I had the miscarriage naturally at home. I was grateful for that.

I grieve for that baby. I always will in certain ways. But I saw the path in front of me, so I kept walking.

It's a thing I both hate and love about myself: my need to keep going. When I hurt and break and bleed, I want to *do* something about it, to change it, to make it better. But so often there is nothing to do. Sometimes you have to just wait and just feel. Sometimes you must just do the work of being present and going through the pain.

My memory of the weeks following the miscarriage will always be hazy. I tried to be there for my daughter, but would I collapse as soon as I tucked her into bed. I went to our family's Thanksgiving dinner, though I did not want to. There were moments I enjoyed, and I even forgot for a minute or two about the loss, but then the pain would come flooding back. There were many tears. Many tarot cards were thrown. Many journal entries were written.

Prior to my miscarriage, I had thought that if I did everything "right," things would turn out OK. But after losing my baby that sense of there being an order to the world was gone. Sometimes a trauma or loss is not merely a roadblock on your way to fulfilling your dreams. Sometimes a trauma or a loss is just that and will never be anything else.

Things got better and worse in small increments. Back and forth, in constant motion, like the ocean's waves.

Trying Again

We decided to try IVF again. The doctor told us the miscarriage had just been bad luck; that the eggs retrieved must have been chromosomally abnormal, which had caused the miscarriage. We still believed we had been led down this path for a reason, and we thought this next cycle might be our lucky one.

The second cycle was much the same as the first. We added a drug or two and changed dosages. And, as with the first time, we ended up with three embryos still growing on day five. We went to the clinic, and I had the two healthiest-looking embryos transferred.

The next day we got a call: the third embryo had stopped growing, so we would have nothing to freeze.

While the process of this second round of IVF was the same, it was much more difficult for me emotionally. Everything seemed to be a trigger and would remind me of the miscarriage: the clinic, the exam room, the ultrasound experience, and especially the waiting. While deep down I was confident IVF would work, I was also extremely anxious and unable to relax.

We survived the 10-day wait for the pregnancy test results. After the blood test. I went back to work thinking I might as well not use up more precious paid time off. Everyone around us thought IVF was going to work. I was cautiously hopeful.

I checked the clinic's patient portal every half hour to see if they had posted the pregnancy test results. This time I would know what the hCG number would mean without a nurse explaining it.

At my desk at work, waiting for my test results, I started to feel like I was having a panic attack. The waiting and my anxiety became overwhelming. I told my boss I needed to work from home. Then I saw the test results pop up in the portal.

The number was eight.

While the clinic technically considered anything over a five to be a positive test result, this was a bad number; it should have been 50–100 or even higher. I felt like I was being punched in the stomach. This was not going to be a viable pregnancy. I was not even going to be able to just mourn and move on because my hCG number was technically positive, so I would have to continue to go through the motions. I kept taking my medications. I kept going in for blood draws. I kept doing all the things I would have been doing if I had been pregnant with a healthy baby.

My hCG numbers went up, but not enough to indicate a viable pregnancy. So, the clinic finally let me stop taking my medication. The doctor determined I was having an early miscarriage.

After more appointments and days of wondering and waiting, I had a second miscarriage.

My heart had been much more guarded this second time around. I also hadn't lived with this pregnancy for weeks, thinking that I would get my baby at the end. I had not had time to become attached. So, I was devastated but not shocked.

I started bleeding on the day of my daughter's fourth birthday party. People asked if I wanted to cancel or reschedule the party, but I felt like it was too late for that, and a distraction seemed like a good idea. It was a beautiful day with blue skies and perfect, white, fluffy clouds. The party was chaotic and fun for the kids, with bubble machines and a bouncy castle. There were moments when I forgot everything that had happened in the past days and weeks.

Perhaps I went overboard with the birthday party, which was one of the many worries I had about our daughter remaining an only child. I did not want to spoil her. I did not want her to feel my sadness or longing as any reflection on her. And I did not want to disappoint her. She was old enough now to want to hold a baby, and in the next few months she would start asking us often if she could have a baby sister.

Next Steps

After my second miscarriage, it was time to meet with the doctor and discuss the next steps. In essence, we had three choices. The first was to try another round of IVF with my own eggs. The second option was to use an egg donor. And the third option was embryo donation. With embryo donation, we would use embryos left over from another couple's successful round of IVF. This would mean there would be no genetic tie to either myself or my husband, but I would be able to carry and deliver the baby.

After enduring two miscarriages in a short amount of time, I really needed some time to process all that had happened. I also needed time to meditate on our next steps. However, we knew there was a waiting list to receive embryos, and it could us take months, or even years, to get to the top. So, we decided to move forward with embryo donation. That way, the clinic could put us on the waiting list for donated embryos.

We are still not entirely sure why, but we moved quickly through the clinic's donation list. We were both elated and completely overwhelmed when the clinic contacted us saying they would send us embryo donor profiles that week.

Choosing embryos felt like a tremendous step, and we were both still grieving. Looking through embryo profiles was difficult for me. I felt good about the road we were on, but not ready to make any big decisions. We had been given an opportunity, though, and we didn't want to throw it away. We went forward with the process.

After a couple of weeks, we made our decision. We ended up choosing the first profile they sent us, which my doctor had chosen for us. It's as if she knew before we did that this was the right match for us.

When we had made that decision, we felt relieved and started making plans to transfer one of the donated embryos. We wanted to first do another laparoscopy to clean out whatever endometriosis had grown since my last surgery so that we could give this little embryo the best chance possible. Our reproductive endocrinologist recommended an excellent surgeon who specialized in endometriosis and understood our fertility-related needs. She was wonderful to work with and made sure we were fully informed and felt good about our plan every step of the way.

They would not perform the surgery for another few months, which gave me time to grieve our loss from the last round of IVF and to fully wrap my head around the next stage of our infertility process.

About six months after a very productive laparoscopic surgery, I started preparing for the transfer. From the beginning, this round felt different. It was easier in every way. I felt calm and much less afraid and anxious. It was much easier physically because we were doing a "natural cycle," meaning I only took a few pills to prepare my body to receive the embryo. We used my body's natural menstrual cycle instead of creating one through injected hormones and medications. The only shot I took the entire cycle was a "trigger shot" so that we could time the transfer correctly. When I was close to ovulation, I went to the clinic every other day to track my uterine lining and make sure the follicle was the correct size. Everything went exactly as planned, and I had the transfer.

Broken and Magical

One year to the day after hearing the words "There's no heart-beat," I woke up to my daughter telling me she had dreamt of her little sister. A lovely, playful dream. It was a busy day, and I didn't remember the anniversary until that night when I was alone. I remembered what my daughter had said that morning and felt some comfort. I still felt the existence of that lost baby. But I felt mostly gratitude for my brief time with that baby, for my daughter in my arms, and for this potential baby.

Even on the anniversary of that first loss, I felt supremely confident about the upcoming transfer. The clinic asked us if we wanted to choose the gender, as the embryos had been chro-mosomally tested. We chose not to. We learned it was a boy after the transfer, during the 10-day wait to find out whether I was pregnant.

On the day of the transfer, I felt that, yes, my body was bro-ken in that it was growing endometrial tissue where it should not. That tissue caused pain and made it very difficult for me to get pregnant. It affected my egg quality. But my body was also magical. It somehow still knew and did just what it was supposed to do when an embryo was transferred to my uterus.

It knew and did what it needed to do to keep my daughter safe when I had a weak placenta that could not support my unborn child until her due date. It created the hormones it was supposed to when it was supposed to make them. My body carried me where I needed to go. It learned and became wiser. It nourished my daughter after she was born. And my body grew a perfect uterine lining and egg follicle for the embryo transfer so that it would be ready to house a little embryo.

I knew my body would not care that someone else produced the egg. It would not matter that there was no genetic tie.

I had never taken an at-home pregnancy test with any of my other transfers. I think I enjoyed prolonging the period in which I could be blissfully pregnant, and I wanted to put off the possibility of bad news. But this time I wanted to take the test. I was sure it would be good news, and I wanted to confirm that as soon as possible.

I took the test. And sure enough, five days after the transfer, I got a light positive result.

Pregnancy after pregnancy loss is difficult. For me, it was stressful and anxiety-producing. Even though my overall confidence in the pregnancy did not fade, fear was always lurking. I took a home pregnancy test every day until my pregnancy blood test at the fertility clinic. I had a slight panic attack every time I thought the line did not show up fast enough. I worried a lot.

One thing that proved to be an enormous source of comfort was buying an at-home Doppler, so that once the heartbeat was strong enough to detect, I could listen to it any time I wanted.

Our son was breech but born safely by cesarean section the week before he was due.

While my path to motherhood did not go quite as I had planned, I can see now that it was still a beautiful path.

While I was pregnant and while we had been pursuing embryo donation, I began reading and thinking about genes and epigenetics and how there is still so much possibility within them. Genes do not necessarily dictate a child's destiny.

While we can't change our actual DNA or that of a donated embryo, I believe we can influence gene expression (that is, the process by which genetic information encoded in a gene is used). For example, proper nutrition and sleep as well as providing affection and security can impact gene expression in our children. The parents we are and the homes we build for our families can actually make a difference not only in our children's personalities but also in their gene expression.

The other day, I was lying between my two precious children, who were both asleep, and feeling so damn lucky. I hoped they could feel my presence as they fell asleep and afterward. I hoped my love and effort would get through to them so that they could take my love and effort wherever they go, and that they would never forget their miraculous beginnings. ■

SUSAN SWEETLAND GARAY is a writer and photographer who currently lives in Oregon's Willamette Valley with her husband and two children where she works in the vineyard industry. She has published three collections of poetry and is also a founding editor of Blue Hour Press which began publishing in 2012. She enjoys spending time in nature with her children, gentle parenting, low toxin living, and being a support for those going through infertility. You can follow her on Instagram @rainwatermama and @tinydancers_embryoadoption.

The Belly of the Whale

KATHERINE HUNTER

"Four hundred and twenty dollars? That has to be a joke!" I screamed, as if taking out my anger on the pharmacy technician would improve my situation.

"I'm sorry, but your insurance company is saying it needs proof that the progesterone is medically necessary," she replied calmly.

That statement, while evidently accurate, did not help calm me down. I started to pipe up again, but then quickly realized an argument would be futile. I would have to appeal the insurance company's decision at a later point.

I handed over my credit card. I would do whatever I needed to do to save my baby and end what my doctor told me was a "threatened abortion." I had been experiencing spotting for more than a week, and while the baby was apparently small, my husband and I had just seen a faint heartbeat at my ultrasound appointment that day. I was seven weeks pregnant with a baby I had desired for a long time, and I needed to do all I could to hold on to him.

My doctor had prescribed progesterone inserts after my natural progesterone levels started to plummet. She said we could be cautiously optimistic. I wasn't optimistic, but I knew that if I didn't pay the $420 for the progesterone, I would regret it.

"This is absolutely ridiculous," I complained. I wanted to tell the pharmacy technician about my problem and everything I'd been through leading up to that moment. She gave me an insincere half-smile and handed me the receipt.

I miraculously summoned the sliver of restraint left inside me, turned around, and hurried out of the store.

As I walked through my apartment door, I felt a gush of blood. I discovered that bright red blood had replaced the intermittent brown spotting. I quickly took the progesterone, but not before hurling some profanities in the universe's direction.

To more fully convey the rage that boiled within me at that moment, a little history is warranted. Let me take you further back.

Infatuated with Mommying

There are many photos of me as a child with some round item stuffed in my shirt, pretending to have a coveted baby in my belly.

I was five years old when my mother and father informed my sister and me that we were going to have another sibling. I was ecstatic. When my baby brother was born, I exulted in playing the role of big sister, helping in every way I could aside from changing dirty diapers.

In elementary school, television episodes that involved the birth of a baby fascinated me (for example, when Jesse and Becky had their twins on *Full House*). I discreetly played with dolls until sixth grade. As I approached middle school, my fascination shifted from being a mom to the awesome experience of being pregnant. I marveled at the female body's ability to grow while carrying and nourishing another human. I was also cognizant of the achievement of giving birth. Surviving the grueling process of childbirth and successfully bringing a human baby into the world is not something that should be discounted, even by American society in the twenty-first century. Now that I'm a mother, I'm even more acutely aware of this fact.

I was 11 when my 31-year-old next-door neighbor told us she was expecting her first child with her husband. I was envious. I scoured baby-name books and ultimately helped them settle on their firstborn's name: Garrett, meaning "spear strength."

As the years passed, more age-appropriate obsessions replaced my infatuation with pregnancy and motherhood: teenage boys, talking to friends on the phone for hours, sneaking into R-rated movies, learning to drive. I was a voracious and competitive babysitter, aspiring to dominate my neighborhood market. I was motivated not by adoration of young children but by earning potential.

As a college student, I strived to remain disciplined and focused (even amid sorority debauchery) on the endgame, which was law school. I wasn't at school to earn an "MRS degree." Rather, I was there to grow, emotionally and intellectually; to augment my mind in various ways; to revel in self-exploration; to attain a degree that would yield financial independence.

Nevertheless, in college, I fortuitously met my now husband-to-be. And as 20-year-olds, we chatted over Long Island Iced Teas about our life aspirations. I matter-of-factly told him I was going to be an attorney, specifically a transactional attorney, partly because of the flexible schedule that I would enjoy as a non-trial lawyer. I wanted to be able to leave the office midday to attend my child's school plays, as my father had done for me. I wanted to be able to work from home when my child was sick.

While I was absorbed in my privileged college lifestyle and genuinely didn't want children for another decade, I still assumed I would be a mother. However, I was oblivious to the strength I would need to muster while traveling my road to motherhood. At that time, I couldn't fathom the arsenal of "spears" I would need to forge through the obstacles I would face. And I was not prepared for the strength I would need to garner to survive the isolation and despair of infertility and pregnancy loss.

Trying and Failing to Get Pregnant

My husband and I, who are the same age, got married at 27. After years of putting the idea of having children on the back burner, the next year I abruptly awakened to my inner yearning to be a mother. However, my husband needed a lot of convincing to start trying to get pregnant. In December 2012, while we were in Peru, we (mainly I) decided to start trying.

No woman can accurately depict her own personality in a few adjectives. Nevertheless, you should know that I have, among other, more endearing traits, neurotic and cynical tendencies. December, January, February, March, and April were stressful and brought out my worst attributes. Some of my friends had started trying to get pregnant, and many had been successful, informing me that it had happened right away, sometimes by accident. One of the first truths you learn when you try to get pregnant and it doesn't happen right away is that those who immediately or accidentally conceive shout about it to the rooftops. Those who struggle are often trying to repress anxiety and don't disclose that they are trying. So, reality *appears* to be that everyone who is trying to get pregnant does right away.

My Google searches concerning how long it takes to get pregnant, and my anxiety around what could be wrong, multiplied rapidly over the next few months. By April, just after five months of trying, I decided I needed to undergo a hysterosalpingography (HSG) test to rule out a fallopian tubal blockage. Endometriosis—which we suspected I had—can cause tubal blockages. Fortunately, my doctor was agreeable to my having an HSG.

The HSG was the most painful procedure I had endured up to that point in my life. And the results were inconclusive: I either had one tube blocked by scar tissue or a uterine spasm had made the fallopian tube fail to be fully visible during the test.

I was devastated and confused. The OBGYN who performed the procedure said, "I'm sorry. You should see a specialist. I can give you a name of a reproductive endocrinologist." And that was it. I left with no definitive answers. I had myriad questions as I spiraled down a dark hole of despair.

Miraculously, a few days later we conceived. Apparently, an HSG can sometimes "clear out" a woman's fallopian tubes, making conception possible, although the test cannot remove scar tissue.

Pregnant for 30 Days

It's cliché, but I felt different. I rushed to the drugstore after work to buy a pregnancy test (sadly, this was not even close to being the first one I'd purchased.) As the cashier, a loquacious middle-aged woman, rang up my purchase, she nonchalantly asked, "Are you hoping the test is positive or negative?" I was shocked. How brazen. I mumbled some answer that I can't remember now. I was angry that she had forced me to answer such a personal question.

I now believe this was just a socially awkward woman trying to make conversation. Perhaps she may have said a silent prayer after asking customers this question, requesting that they would get the "right" result.

Trying to get pregnant had clearly left me cynical and defensive. In the months ahead, an even more angry and pessimistic Katherine would emerge. But at that moment all I knew was that the pregnancy test result might be positive, and I was dying to find out.

I rushed home and took the test. The line indicating I was pregnant appeared quickly. I instantly thought of a baby boy. My baby boy.

It was a three-day weekend, and my husband had left for an out-of-town bachelor party. I couldn't tell anyone, even my mother, before telling him! And I did not want to share such monumental news over the phone, so I kept the secret.

I immediately calculated my due date: January 8, 2014. I was giddy. I started pinning pictures of nurseries to my private Pinterest board and scouring Craigslist for a new apartment in Chicago (where we would be moving from Evanston soon), since we would now be needing space for a nursery.

When my husband returned home, I secretly recorded myself sharing the news with him. I have only been able to bring myself to watch that video once since that day, and it took a long time to muster the strength to do so. The video has since become lost, but I've held on to what that baby inside me for 30 days meant.

I knew I was pregnant for only two weeks before it became apparent that something was wrong. I started to see brown spotting. Everyone said to not be alarmed, but I was. I had had a bad feeling all along, as if I knew the pregnancy was too good to be true. I pushed those feelings aside, trying to revel in the excitement. When the spotting started, my heart sunk. After a few days, it really picked up. I was alone in Kansas City house sitting while my parents were in Europe. I eventually found the courage to go to an urgent care, which contacted a local OBGYN who was willing to perform an ultrasound and do blood work. The ultrasound showed a fetal pole and fetal sac, but no heartbeat was detected. The doctor told me not to panic; that my dating might be off and, therefore, it was too soon to detect a heartbeat. I left the office relieved that there was no ectopic pregnancy, as Dr. Google had told me sometimes occurs after an HSG.

When I got home, though, I started to realize that this news was not good because I *had* tracked my dates with precision. I was definitely six weeks pregnant.

Leading up to a follow-up appointment with my OBGYN in Evanston, my husband and I had an intense fight. All the stress and anxiety we'd felt for the past five months while trying to get pregnant, compounded by anxiety about the prospect of now losing the pregnancy, was too much to handle. This was a dark time for me personally and for our marriage. Nevertheless, we walked hand in hand to the appointment, me certain we were going to see no heartbeat and my husband hopeful that we would.

My husband's wishful thinking proved successful for the time being. There was a faint heartbeat, but the fetus was too small for seven weeks of gestation. The doctor explained we should be cautiously optimistic. She then handed me a prescription for progesterone to help sustain the pregnancy for at least a week longer, at which point I would have another ultrasound. After handing over $420 for the progesterone, I rushed home to start the medication, only to find that bright red blood had now replaced the intermittent brown spotting. Any sliver of optimism that I had tried to maintain started to rapidly vanish.

After what seemed like an eternity, at eight weeks pregnant, I had another ultrasound. I had experienced quite a bit of cramping by that point, and the bleeding had picked up in the past week. This ultrasound was to confirm what we already knew. We were in the waiting room of the Fetal Medicine department at the hospital, surrounded by visibly pregnant women. I was a mess. As I later wrote in my journal, at that moment I had wanted the pregnant women in the waiting room "to vanish into f#&@ing thin air."

They called my name, and the ultrasound was quickly over. There was no heartbeat. They were sorry. I left with a prescription for a medication to initiate a miscarriage and a painkiller. (Many women end up having a dilation and curettage (D&C), a surgical procedure that can occasionally lead to complications. I am grateful my doctor did not insist on a D&C because it wasn't necessary.)

I didn't know what to expect. Other than my mom more than 30 years earlier, I didn't know anyone who had had a miscarriage. I popped the pills and sat on the couch with my computer, again resorting to handy Google, searching for clues about what would follow but not finding much information on what a miscarriage was like.

Here's what miscarriage felt like for me:

I sat on the couch with my dog and husband watching TV and had mild cramping. I was sullen, but I was also relieved that the limbo was over and I would soon be able to start the healing process. The cramping got worse about four hours after taking the medication. I passed a lot of blood. The cramping came in waves, often starting in my back and sweeping around my lower abdomen for what seemed to be more than a minute at a time. I now know that this pain was the same pain that women experience during labor. At times I had to lie on the floor, ironically in a fetal position, to ease the pain from the contractions. My dog was frantic about not being able to help. I took a narcotic painkiller, which numbed the pain considerably. The blood continued to pick up. Seven hours after taking the medication, I started to feel nauseated and like there was pressure in my pelvis. I felt the urge to urinate, and when I did, my body expelled the fetal pole, followed by a dark clot (the placenta) nearly the size of a golf ball. It was all a bit shocking for sure, but I was mostly unemotional. The emotions would flare up again soon enough.

Trying Again (Times 12)

Not enough people are aware of how significant the healing process after childbirth is, how much time is needed to recover fully, both physically and mentally, and how unpleasant the healing process can be. Generally speaking, American society does not offer the support system that new mothers need. (I could write a separate book about that.)

But what about those of us whose bodies gear up to carry a baby for nine months and then evict the baby prematurely? We are invisible. Our stories are not well known. Our suffering is not typically shared. And we get no baby as a consolation prize.

For more than two weeks after my miscarriage, I shuffled through life with a gigantic menstrual pad between my legs. The pad served as a steadfast reminder of a trauma I wanted to forget; a trauma from which I desperately wanted to leap forward. The bleeding was intense at times. I had to go to the doctor once a week to have my blood tested to see if my human chorionic gonadotropin (hCG) levels were dropping sufficiently. I also had to keep sorting through—and paying—new medical bills I received for the pregnancy-related ultrasounds, medications, and doctor's appointments. A small victory occurred when the insurance company granted my appeal and reimbursed the full $420 I had paid for the progesterone inserts.

During this time, I would vacillate between genuinely trying to propel myself forward and feeling so low and empty that I could not stand to get out of bed. In hindsight, I probably experienced something similar to postpartum depression.

I started a blog. Checked that off of my to-do list. At first, it was simply about my interests at the time: cooking, traveling, and reading. Then, about a month after the miscarriage, I wrote four posts documenting my miscarriage experience. The blog was cathartic to say the least, although I kept it private and password protected. I dabbled in yoga and meditation. I wrote a work-related article. I made acupuncture appointments. I channeled nervous energy into buying furniture and decor to make a fresh start in the Chicago townhouse where we'd be moving at the end of the summer (which had an empty bedroom because we no longer needed a nursery).

Yet I couldn't shake the morose feelings. I kept having crying spells. I grieved for the life I had carried inside me and wept for the baby I had thought I would hold, rock, and watch grow into a child, teenager, and adult. I held pity parties to which I invited my husband and mother, and, occasionally, friends. I truly felt that no one could help me, and I would allow no one to try. No one could understand what I was going through unless they themselves had lost a pregnancy (or at least that was how I felt). My dog was my most steadfast companion and trusted confidant during this dark time. She didn't judge me or offer unsolicited advice; instead, her unconditional love showed up for me each day and she frequently—knowingly and quietly—sat by my side for hours, as I would cry and nap on my couch.

My anger during this period was intense and blinding. My husband walked on eggshells, and others started to do so as well. Both my mother and husband tried to help me to see that things could be so much worse, to focus on gratitude, and to realize that no harm could come from positive thinking. I wasn't having it. I was still in the anger stage of grief, and I can assure you that grief is not linear. It was the stage in which I remained the longest, and even when I thought I had moved ahead, it would resurface with a vengeance.

Those close to me came to realize that they could not force healing on me, nor could they understand the depths of my despair. They never knew what would set me off. A few things would, without question: a visibly pregnant woman having the audacity to be within 500 feet of me, getting an invitation to a baby shower, and, lastly, being asked when I was going to have a baby. If I dissect the rage, I was primarily angry about and frustrated by the fact that life is not fair and I had no control over whether I was going to achieve the role of mother for which I so pined. I was angry that I didn't have my baby while other women had no trouble getting pregnant. Beneath the anger, I also felt insecure and embarrassed. My life experience had taught me that hard work usually pays off, so I found it unsettling to be failing when I was trying so hard.

Seemingly ordinary interactions presented obstacles. I found myself avoiding friends, old colleagues, and acquaintances because I didn't know how to respond to the "How are you?" and "What's new?" questions, or the most dreaded of all, which came in multifaceted versions: "When are you going to start having kids?" Even strangers asking "Do you have kids?" left such a sting; the question served as a reminder of my pain.

A part of me wanted to divulge everything, but that would have left me too vulnerable. I became an unreliable friend. I would cancel plans at the last minute because I would get my period, receive discouraging medical news, or feel too sullen after someone around me announced their pregnancy. Some days, I couldn't bear to be around anyone. I found it difficult to plan the future—and I am a planner with a capital P. For example, it was tricky to know if I should book a vacation with friends or attend an out-of-town wedding or a bachelorette party because I didn't know with certainty what time of the month I would be most fertile, whether I would be pregnant by the time the wedding came around, or whether I'd be going through a fertility treatment. I would make excuses for not attending baby showers and first birthday parties; I just couldn't bring myself to feign happiness. I would then be consumed by guilt for having these negative feelings.

The distractions of a busy work life—and time—started to chip away at the thick layer of anger that had consumed me for several months. While the anger lifted, I started to experience more happy moments, and I had fewer melancholy days. However, no matter what distraction I concocted, I was unsuccessful at managing the underlying anxiety. Anxiety about how I still wasn't pregnant. Anxiety about what could be wrong. Anxiety about how many friends were going to be pregnant soon. Anxiety about what my would-have-been due date would be like.

The holidays were approaching, and my husband and I would soon be driving seven hours to spend Christmas in his hometown. I had imagined an entirely different scenario when I had found out I was pregnant months earlier. I thought I would be weeks away from delivering our first child—the first grandchild on both sides—so we'd be spending Christmas with our families, cozied up in our Chicago townhouse merrily awaiting our miracle baby's debut. I'd been looking forward to having an excuse to not travel for the holidays, too.

Finally, January 8, 2014, arrived. It was one of the most brutally cold days that winter, with a wind chill of nearly negative 40. I did not go to the office because of the cold. A feeling of dread settled in my belly, where my baby was supposed to be. I knew, though, that I had to face the day. In an effort to do so, I wrote the following blog post dedicated to him:

> At first, I could not wait for this day to arrive. The date carried so much potential and offered such hope. It would have been the date (or around the date) that I would have met you for the

first time. Before you left me, I had already thought about your name, what you would look like, what kind of relationship you and I might have. But, as your very essence would soon teach me, things don't always work out the way we intend for them to work out; life does not usually happen as we envision it will, or as we expect it will, or how we think it should.

For many, many months I have dreaded this date. I woke up today and grief nearly consumed me. But this day is here and although a part of me wants to run and hide from it, I know that I have to own it. The pain that this journey has caused me has already helped redefine me, has challenged me, has forever altered the fabric of my being, and has helped me to grow in ways that I desperately needed to grow. You did that for me and I will never, ever forget you. If there is a God—and candidly I will admit that many days I have questioned whether there is—then you were sent to me by God, to be the impetus that has forced me to open my eyes, and I will eternally be grateful to you for what you have taught me. You are my angel.

But why could you not have taught me to be more empathetic, to make meaning out of tragedy, to be more thoughtful, to be a better listener, to be kinder, right here on Earth? Why couldn't you have been born and helped me realize that there is so much that I have no control over, or helped to strengthen the bond I have with my husband? Why did your heartbeat have to stop?

I will never know. I don't like that, and I abhor all of the bullshit that accompanies a miscarriage, but I am (very) slowly learning to accept all of this.

My heart is heavy knowing that I will never meet you—not today or any day. And I am so sorry that your heartbeat stopped. I feel responsible. Please know that I wanted you so

> badly. I already loved you before I knew you were going to leave me. I wrote to you and thought of you often. But none of that mattered.
>
> You do matter, though, and you will forever mean so much to me. January 8 will always be your day. I believe I will think of you and your enormous impact on my life for the rest of my days, but especially on your day. I vow that each January 8 for the rest of my life I will honor you in some way.

I also made a contribution to the Chicago Botanic Garden in his honor; the gardens would plant a flower for him in the spring. My best friend sent me a handmade glass ornament to remember the baby by, and another sent me a text message saying she was thinking of me. She had a five-month-old, and I hadn't spoken to her in months. She remembered my due date, and that touched me.

As I went to bed, I was relieved that the day had come to an end. It hadn't been nearly as bad as I had anticipated. Anticipation is half the battle. I would wake up on January 9 with a more healed heart. I could more fully focus on the road ahead.

I became laser-focused on getting pregnant and staying pregnant. After the miscarriage, my husband and I had been trying for five months. Five long months, yet it wasn't even half a year. I wanted to be pregnant yesterday, not tomorrow. Each time my period arrived, I became more discouraged and disheartened than the previous month.

I can now see that five months of trying to conceive is not, in fact, an eternity. However, I still recall the turmoil I experienced during those five months. If some generous soul had bestowed on me the gift of a crystal ball, I could have survived my infertility journey free of agony. I would have known that at some point, I would, in fact, become a mother. During those months, I allowed my fear of never becoming a mom to nestle its way into my mind. And this fear did not loosen its grip; it gripped more tightly as each month passed.

By December 2013, I wanted to see a reproductive endocrinologist. Objectively, I must have appeared impatient, and there were tenets of truth to this judgment. However, I believed I probably had endometriosis, which can make conceiving very difficult. In 2013, not as much was known about endometriosis, including its causes, and to diagnose it with certainty required surgery. I was told by more than one doctor that the surgery itself could cause damage, and even if the endometrial tissue were successfully removed, it would likely grow back.

When my husband and I arrived for our first visit with the reproductive endocrinologist, his first words centered on the fact that I was about 10 years younger than his average patient. This frustrated me. I said pointedly that despite my age, I still very much hoped to get pregnant and have more than one child. He surmised that I likely had a tubal blockage on one side, but he was optimistic about my prospects of conceiving with the other "clear" tube. To increase my chances of producing more than one follicle each month (and one on the clear side), he prescribed a low dose of Clomid.

Clomid is the devil's drug. It made me very moody and caused insomnia, and when I was able to sleep, I would wake up drenched from night sweats. I tried Clomid for two months. During both months, I produced a follicle on my presumed blocked side. I couldn't take Clomid for a third month because I had developed an ovarian cyst, which is another unpleasant side effect of Clomid.

So, my husband and I again tried on our own. We were again unsuccessful.

In Vitro Fertilization

By April 2014, we had started down the road of in vitro fertilization (IVF).

I know many couples prefer to try every possible alternative before embarking on IVF. They want to avoid its astounding costs, the potent injectable drugs that must be administered, the intense monitoring (daily blood work and ultrasounds, retrieval schedules, transfer schedules), and the potentially serious side effects of the drugs. I very much respect the approach to exhaust other options before trying IVF, as well as the decision to avoid it altogether if it doesn't feel right.

Several stories in this book include a happy ending that circumvented IVF. I, however, did not feel that the next step (intrauterine insemination) would be fruitful because of my likely diagnosis of tubal blockage or endometriosis. The prospects for success with IVF seemed pretty good given my husband's and my ages. Candidly, part of what made me willing to try IVF was my insurance coverage. We had a fully insured health plan subject to Illinois state insurance law, which required coverage of fertility treatments. Jumping to IVF next made sense to me, and I was eager to do it. We were young with a likely tubal infertility diagnosis (the type that IVF was invented to address), and we had insurance coverage. The likely successful outcome outweighed the financial costs, as well as the figurative costs associated with stabbing myself with needles and subjecting myself to a physically brutal process.

Thankfully, our reproductive endocrinologist was receptive to my request to try IVF. My husband and I scheduled an IVF orientation at a clinic, during which we watched videos on how to administer injectable medications, met with a psychologist to discuss the rigors of the process, and learned more about what IVF entails. I left the appointment feeling energized and hopeful. My husband left feeling more overwhelmed because he had not been as familiar with IVF. I had done my research. I had read blogs and talked to friends of friends who had done it ("safe" people to contact; I did not want any of my friends or family knowing we were trying IVF because if it failed I wanted to disclose the defeat on my own terms, in my own time).

The IVF process was grueling. When I went back and read my notes and journal entries in preparation for writing this book, I realized I had forgotten the minute details, including the emotional toll of undergoing IVF took on me.

I am a Type A-er without question, so I had expectations of what *should* happen all mapped out. What *did* happen was that the IVF clinic miscalculated dates, my ovaries decided to produce a cyst, and my body didn't respond to the medications right away. Yet we finally made it over all the hurdles to the egg retrieval.

Ten eggs were retrieved, and all 10 were fertilized. Solid numbers. Yet after three days of growing in the lab, the embryos started to fizzle. The usual hope is to get to day five (the blastocyst stage) before transferring an embryo to the uterus, but my doctor rushed me on day three to transfer one of the embryos that looked "good."

I was very pessimistic that the one embryo would implant and develop into a healthy baby that my body would be able to carry for nine months. The source of my pessimism was multifactorial. I knew enough to know that 10 fertilized eggs fizzling by day three was concerning. So, I had my doubts that this one embryo was of good quality, especially in light of my earlier miscarriage. And from there, I allowed my fear to snowball. My typical approach is to prepare for the worst and hope for the best, and the past 17 months of infertility and a pregnancy loss had left me more pessimistic than ever. I wasn't particularly unhealthy, but there was always room for improvement. And I feared that something in my past—whether it was Accutane I took in my twenties, a horrid diet as a child (I subsisted on cheese, bread, and some fruit for two decades), or a wastewater facility near my childhood neighborhood that may have been correlated with people developing cancer—had deteriorated my egg quality. I had allowed the past 17 months to leave me in a deep state of self-hatred. I loathed my body for not being able to do what, in my mind, every woman should be able to do: make, carry, and birth a baby. While human conception, pregnancy, and childbirth are, in fact, miraculous feats, it seemed from my vantage point at the time that these processes were easy for many women.

And, in fact, IVF didn't work. I did technically get pregnant, but I didn't stay pregnant. My hCG levels were very, very low (12.5). Most home pregnancy tests will not register a positive result until hCG is 25. I ended up having to go in for multiple blood tests and multiple ultrasounds, just as I'd done nearly a year earlier. And just as with that first experience, at eight weeks, the ultrasound finally confirmed what I already knew: no heartbeat.

Spear strength swept over me almost instantly. I was not going to let this impending miscarriage suck me into a deep, dark hole of self-pity, rage, and depression like the last one had. My soul—and my marriage—could not withstand that again. I would stoically move forward and request medication for a miscarriage. I would grit my teeth and endure the miscarriage. I would grieve, I would yell, I would cry, but I would not allow myself to linger idly in a pit of despair for too long. I was going to find some way to move forward, although I didn't yet know what moving forward would look like or how I was going to do it.

Making Use of the Time Inside the Whale

The day after my second miscarriage I took the day off from work. I went to the Chicago Botanic Garden and just meandered. I didn't know what I was supposed to feel. I needed some direction. A sign. What was I supposed to do? Try to transfer our remaining embryo, knowing very well that I could be right back where I was? Should we explore adoption more seriously? Should I meditate more on what life without kids would look like and if it could be the life for us? Perhaps we should explore IVF options at a different, more adept clinic?

When I returned home, my beloved *Real Simple* magazine had arrived. I opened it to find this quote:

> Rest is not idleness, and to lie sometimes on the grass under the trees on a summer's day, listening to the murmur of water, or watching the clouds float across the blue sky, is by no means a waste of time.
>
> —*John Lubbock*

Those words offered me some comfort. Later in the day, I ran across a blog post that ultimately helped me develop the mantra that would get me through the rest of my infertility journey. The author was symbolically comparing herself to the

Biblical character Jonah and her infertility journey to the time spent in the "belly of the whale." She urged readers to consider what they planned to do with the "belly time" in light of her conviction that this time would come to an end. It was up to us to decide how we wanted to spend that time (as well as the time once we were out of the belly).

This analogy left me with a sliver of clarity. I felt motivated to find meaning in my wait. The resolve to live more fully, and to endure my wait more gracefully, strengthened over the next few days. I resisted my natural inclination to want immediate answers. I started a dialogue in my head that went something like this:

> I really need to, up to a point, start accepting and even embracing my wait. I can listen to what the universe is suggesting I do next without having to make a decision right away. I can still actively try to seek answers during my wait, but I don't need to be so forceful with such attempts. I can seek answers in a more graceful, patient manner.

I slowly found myself settling into a calmer place. A place of calmer waters, one might say. A place where I was more content waiting. I started to embrace the wait, knowing that answers likely would not appear for quite a while, but that I needed to wait and see what time would reveal. For so many months I had been trying to avoid my "belly of the whale time," trying with all my might to push it away. I had unquestionably been enduring a stormy chapter of my life. My time in the belly of the whale was inevitable. I was there, like it or not, and my quest to get out quickly had not served me well or yielded many answers.

I also started to recall the words my mother had been saying and writing to me for the past year: "You have so very little control over the outcome of your wait, but you do have control over how you wait and what you do with this wait."

This wait, my time in the belly of the whale, was most likely my saving grace, my most teachable moment up to that point. The transformation of perspective unraveling within me ultimately caused me to use my wait to focus more deeply on my connections with others. In particular, I was able to find a deeper connection with my husband. I also worked on my relationship with myself, and I cannot underscore the importance of this work enough.

Over the next few months, my husband and I planned some trips, we volunteered at a local animal shelter, and we started exploring ethnic restaurants in Chicago. I started taking fiddle lessons. I started blogging more. I read more. I took more bubble baths. I went on more dates with my husband. I tried to connect with my friends (those without kids) with more sincerity.

All the while, I kept pushing forward, trying to find answers, soaking up information, and meditating on what the next step should be, but in a less frantic fashion. My husband and I talked with two new doctors, one at a well-known clinic in Colorado with impressive success rates and another at a clinic in Chicago that I knew about from acquaintances. We brought our current doctor a list of questions, which we felt were inadequately answered. I read several eye-opening books about fertility. I talked with my acupuncturist about lifestyle changes. We didn't have definitive answers about what was going on with us, but it was possible we had both egg and sperm quality issues, in addition to my presumed endometriosis.

We decided to make lifestyle changes we felt would benefit our overall health, even if they didn't result in a baby. We both took supplements correlated with (according to some research) better egg and sperm quality. We abstained from alcohol and significantly limited our caffeine intake. We changed our diets to incorporate fertility-friendly foods.

Success

On September 2, 2014, I talked by phone with a woman (I had never met) named Sarah. She was a coach at my husband's gym, where it had somehow come up that she had conceived through IVF. My husband urged me to call Sarah to learn about her experience with the clinic we were considering. She had used the same clinic and doctor we were considering using if we tried IVF again. She was nine months pregnant thanks to IVF and was scheduled to deliver her daughter the next day.

I wasn't convinced I could endure the IVF experience again. However, we were thinking it might make sense to try again at a different clinic, one with a better lab and medical team, than try to transfer the one embryo we had frozen at the first IVF clinic. The IVF process had frustrated us at the first clinic, which had an unorganized staff and subpar lab. Another reason for trying IVF again at a different clinic was that even if they transferred an embryo and we got a baby out of it, we would likely have to try IVF again to have a subsequent child.

Sarah told me about her experience at the clinic, which was generally positive. She urged me to be aggressive about trying to have a baby and to not delay.

I have often reflected on this day, this conversation with Sarah. Perfect timing is an odd, human-concocted idea,

I suppose. Were her words The Truth? I don't know, but they were the truth I needed to hear that day. I had been teetering for a while, waiting for a sign before making a final decision about the next stepping stone. Her words served as the push I needed to proceed forward. Had we not had that conversation when we had it, I would not have the children I have today.

When I listen to and observe my children, and when they challenge me in important ways, I have no doubt that they are the children I was meant to parent. My children are the reason I have more faith than ever that a God does exist. (And I wouldn't rule out the possibility that this God played a hand in orchestrating my conversation with Sarah.) My first miscarriage set the stage for a metamorphosis within me. But I wasn't ready yet for the full transformation. I wouldn't have been the mother I am today had that first baby made his way into my arms. I know that with certainty now.

A few weeks later, I was again injecting IVF drugs into my thighs and buttocks. It was not fun, but I got through it. The doctor retrieved nine eggs and eight were fertilized. We had the eight embryos, plus the one from the previous clinic, tested for chromosomal abnormalities. All nine were chromosomally normal, which was incredible, and starkly different from the results of our first IVF round. We now had nine perfect embryos frozen in time. All we needed was a healthy and receptive uterus.

The next month I had two embryos transferred. My body absorbed one (a boy). But with some fanfare, I imagine, my uterus welcomed the other into its lining, where that microscopic, miraculous embryo proceeded to grow for nine months.

I'm not sure words can ever accurately capture the grandeur of a baby's birth. Or maybe I just cannot find the words that bring justice to the magnificence of the moment my first child was born. To wrap up my story, though, I'll try.

The moment the doctor pulled my daughter from my body, I mistakenly thought the umbilical cord was a penis. For most of my pregnancy, I had convinced myself that I was carrying a sweet boy (perhaps because I so wanted to have a daughter that I was mentally preparing myself for a son). As the doctor placed her on my chest, my husband whispered in my ear "It's a girl." With those words, a flood of emotion swept over me, the chief being sheer joy. "I cannot believe she is here," I kept saying over and over. Yet here she was, a product of eastern and western medicine; a product of intense desire and yearning; a product of determination; a product of tears, grit, meditation, and hope; a product of a community effort that offered us collaboration, fellowship, and emotional support; and perhaps a product of successful prayer.

My path to motherhood had come to an end, and I was embarking on the most rewarding path yet traveled: the path *of* motherhood. My journey to motherhood was challenging, but it was also revelatory and significant and a journey that, in hindsight, I wouldn't change if given the chance. It has come to be a journey for which I am genuinely grateful.

I am also proud to be a member of a community of women who struggled to get pregnant. We are warriors. My infertility is my badge of honor. No other single event or experience has come close to changing me in such a monumental (and positive) manner. The experience of infertility has made me a better spouse, a more empathetic soul, and a more thoughtful and devoted friend. It is what has made me the best parent I can be. Motherhood for me is unquestionably the fruit of a yearning—a yearning that my infertility journey intensified—and my children are the benefactors of a sweeter fruit because of this deep yearning.

May your suffering—your time in the belly of the whale—ultimately weave its way through your most victorious and meaningful love story, as has been the case for me. ■

KATHERINE HUNTER lives in St. Louis, Missouri, with her husband, three children, and dog. She is an employee benefits (ERISA) attorney. When time allows, Katherine enjoys reading American fiction, exploring the St. Louis restaurant scene, exercising, traveling, and cooking. She feels passionate about helping homeless animals, improving the environment, and bringing awareness to challenges associated with infertility. You can contact her at pathstomotherhood@gmail.com.

Worth It All

MEGAN PALMER

Buzz. Buzz. The glass screen on my phone lights up the dark bedroom as it vibrates my nightstand and I glance at the clock. It's 6:08 a.m. I've been awake for hours. Waiting all night for this phone call, from a number I don't recognize, and yet I know who is calling.

Waiting five endless days since my latest egg retrieval.

Waiting five excruciating months since our last failed round of IVF.

Waiting five long years since we decided to turn our family of two into three.

So much waiting.

You might think I wouldn't have wanted to wait a second more, but I hesitated before answering the call from the embryologist.

I will bring you back to 6:08 a.m. later in this story. But I first must explain why I hesitated before answering the call.

All I could think about was the last time I had answered this call, five months earlier on a snowy morning. On that winter morning five months earlier I had been full of hope and ready to hear how many embryos had survived and could be frozen and tested. I was also anxious and scared to hear the news. Especially given that "diminished ovarian reserve" was my diagnosis and the assumed source of our five years of struggle with infertility.

Yet our doctor had remained optimistic, so I did as well.

That is, until I answered the call from the embryologist on that snowy winter morning, at roughly the same hour. I wasn't prepared for what I heard: only one embryo had survived to day five, and it wasn't high enough quality to freeze and test.

I was in shock and didn't even know the right questions to ask. I said thank you and hung up.

My husband looked at me with an expectant smile and asked what they had told me.

"None. We didn't get a single one."

The tears started flowing and would not stop for days.

Leading Up to This Moment

That day, watching the snow fall softly outside, I sat and thought about the previous five years. We had started out like any couple. We were married at ages 28 and 29 and figured we were ready to start trying for a family, as we knew several couples for whom it had taken a little longer than they anticipated to get pregnant.

At my annual physical, my primary care physician and I had discussed my going off of birth control and trying to get pregnant. As she talked about how long it might take for the birth control to stop having an effect, she suddenly stopped massaging my thyroid.

"Have you had any trouble swallowing lately?" she asked.

I assured her I hadn't. My back stiffened, and my heart raced. This was not the line of questioning I wanted during a routine exam—especially one at which we had been discussing getting pregnant.

She felt a small lump on my thyroid and wanted me to follow up with an ultrasound. "It's probably nothing," she said. Oh, and one more thing: I should hold off on discontinuing birth control "just in case."

I was furious; why did I have to wait to come back for an ultrasound when something so big had just been dropped on me? I now know this was merely the genesis of my days of waiting (impatiently).

A week later I went in for the thyroid ultrasound. The technician seemed extremely optimistic. However, I needed to wait for the doctor to see the results.

Again, I waited. Two weeks passed and I heard nothing. Finally, I called. I waited a few more days for a return call. I figured that if something had been wrong, they would have called me right away.

I was certainly not expecting what came next: my doctor telling me that the ultrasound was inconclusive and I needed a biopsy.

Yet more waiting. First to schedule the biopsy and then for the day to arrive.

And then obtaining the biopsy results required—you guessed it—*more waiting.*

Then the results again came back inconclusive. My doctor wanted me to see an ear, nose and throat (ENT) specialist to determine whether my thyroid needed to be removed.

Fast forward a month and I found myself staring at the ceiling of an exam room again, being prepped for surgery.

Fortunately, I don't remember much about the surgery. After a night in the hospital, they sent me home to heal. I had a large incision across my neck covered with bandages, serious nausea, crazy body temperature swings, zero energy, and moderate pain. What I didn't have was any information about my thyroid; I had to wait for the results, of course.

A week later I returned to my job as a teacher.

At the end of the day, several of my teacher friends decided I needed a distraction while waiting to hear from my doctor. So, we headed to a happy hour that included fishbowl-sized beverages. I sucked down a giant margarita as my colleagues attempted to make me laugh.

As I was getting home, my doctor finally called. He apologized for not getting back to me for so long. His soft voice was filled with concern. I knew that signaled bad news. The surgery had revealed malignant cells—the nodule had been cancerous. The good news was that he'd taken my entire thyroid out and that the nodule had not spread to other areas of my thyroid, so technically, my cancer was gone. His office would contact me regarding the next treatment steps.

After three unreturned phone calls to my ENT's office, someone finally answered, and I found out I needed a referral to an endocrinologist for "radioactive treatment." I figured that would happen immediately. Cancer meant urgency, right?

Wrong.

The nurse said she'd send the referral and someone would call from the endocrinologist's office. After more than a week, a scheduler called me back; she was confused about the urgency in my voice—hadn't they told me I needed to wait at least six weeks in between surgery and the RAI treatment? I wasn't sure what RAI was, and nobody had mentioned a six-week wait.

I thought I was devastated after that phone call, but I had no idea what was coming.

After the first of oh-so-many blood tests, I met with my endocrinologist. Even though the cancer was technically gone, she wanted to ensure that no other thyroid cells remained that could turn cancerous.

I would undergo radioactive iodine treatment (RAI) by swallowing a dose of radioactive iodine that would get sucked up by any remaining thyroid cells, which would then be destroyed by the radioactivity. I'd first have to follow a strict low iodine diet for six weeks. After taking the RAI, I would need to self-isolate for a week. And oh, she threw in at the end: if you're thinking of getting pregnant, you'll have to wait a year to allow the radioactivity to leave your body. We wouldn't want the RAI to attack the fetus' thyroid tissues as they developed.

Hold on, what?

I could deal with a stringent diet even if it was no fun and I could read books and watch television on my own for a week, but what I had been told was going to be an easy treatment suddenly turned into something much worse. Six months ago I had visited my doctor to discuss going off birth control to start trying for a family. And now I was learning it would be an entire year before we could even start trying to conceive. I cried uncontrollably in the doctor's office and on and off for days after that. I'm sure everyone thought it was about the cancer, and probably some of it was. But deep down I knew I was going to go from a 29-year-old who wanted to get pregnant for the first time to at least a 31-year-old coming off of cancer treatment without a baby, and that had me thinking worst-case scenario.

Thus began another constant in my life in addition to more waiting: fear.

Fast forward to a year later and I was finally cancer-free. I then waited six months for a second RAI dose to leave my body.

And then I was finally "cleared for pregnancy."

Cleared for Pregnancy

So, you're probably thinking, OK, that's a nice/depressing/confusing story about cancer, but what does that have to do with infertility and early morning phone calls from embryologists?

According to all of my doctors—my primary care doctor, ENT, endocrinologist, OBGYN, and eventually even my fertility specialists—it shouldn't have anything to do with it. The RAI was safe; I didn't need to freeze or protect my eggs, and my fertility wouldn't be affected since it only targeted the thyroid cells. And after my thyroidectomy, my endocrinologist had put me on a synthetic thyroid hormone (Synthroid) and we'd spent many months adjusting my dosage to perfect my thyroid-stimulating hormone (TSH) levels. Yet to this day, I still have trouble believing that my cancer treatment didn't play a significant role in my infertility journey (beyond prolonging the time when we could start trying to get pregnant).

Once I was cleared to try to get pregnant, my OBGYN warned me it could take several months for the birth control to stop being effective. I was only 31, she said. I had plenty of time. I should let her know at my next yearly appointment if we had any issues; I'd undoubtedly be in before then with a positive pregnancy test.

I left her office trying to keep my hope and optimism afloat in my sea of fear.

I went home and downloaded the Ovia fertility app to my phone. I bought my first box of pregnancy tests and tried not to think too much about it as the fall days went by.

After three months of tracking and trying with no luck, I got a little concerned. That pool of fear started to bubble up a bit. I told myself to stay positive and keep trying. When I saw a birth announcement from a high school friend on Facebook, I smiled. That would be us soon, I thought. I congratulated her and bought my first box of ovulation tests.

Six more months went by and nothing. Every month I was tracking everything from ovulation and intercourse to the thickness of my vaginal mucus, something I never thought I'd enter into an app. Every interminable month of waiting got more painful than the last, as my period kept arriving.

It was that waiting again. It was driving me crazy, and there was nothing I could do to speed up the process.

As the number of months trying turned to double digits, my anxiety increased exponentially with each passing month. In the back of my mind, I had a bad feeling that getting pregnant wasn't going to be easy for us. I don't know why. Maybe it was the randomness of my thyroid cancer (no genetic tie or environmental exposure cause). But as October came back around and my yearly OBGYN appointment arrived, I was in full panic mode.

That year I had decided to try to take control of my health, so I had made a few lifestyle changes. After tracking my vitals on an app, taking ovulation tests, losing weight, eating healthier foods, and doing regular exercise, all I had to show for it was 12 months' worth of negative pregnancy tests.

Diagnosing the Issue(s)

I headed to my annual OBGYN appointment with dread. My doctor listened to my concerns as I held back tears, and, accordingly, she ordered some blood tests.

That was it? A year of trying for pregnancy with no success and she ordered blood tests? I was 32 and all I could think about was the movie *Look Who's Talking* in which Kirstie Alley's doctor warns her about her biological clock ticking and she has nightmares about a giant clock. I didn't necessarily dream about evil timepieces chasing me, but that pool of fear was getting deeper by the day.

I kept my phone next to me every minute of the day that week until it finally rang with the results. The tests revealed nothing significantly abnormal.

My doctor recommended I continue doing what I was doing, and she'd send me a referral to a fertility specialist to perform further tests on my husband and me.

I hung up and realized that it had never occurred to me that the problem could be on my husband's end. It could even be, the nurse had said, us both.

The referral to a fertility specialist took several weeks to obtain, and then it was the holidays, and the clinic was booked a month out for new patients. Finally, in mid-February, we had our first appointment with the fertility specialist.

We sat in a pastel-colored waiting room filled with white chairs: relaxing instrumental music played softly in the background, and a screen displayed inspirational quotes about perseverance and strength in the face of adversity.

One woman came through the door, waved at the receptionist, who obviously recognized her, and breezed back into the lab. A few minutes later, she emerged, waving again, saying hello to a nurse by name as she left. I was astounded by how comfortable she was there and how everyone seemed to know her.

I had no idea how much I would resemble that woman later that year.

Our first appointment was fairly straightforward.

The nurses and doctor explained potential issues—everything from ovarian reserve and sperm count to age and medical history. I now finally had a medical team that was wasting no time; I would be 33 that summer.

My husband went off to deposit his specimen, which would be sent for testing right away.

I found myself on an exam table, a sheet across my lap, feet in stirrups, and ready for my first vaginal ultrasound. I stared at the ceiling, taking deep breaths and attempting to change my mindset from fear to excitement. After all, the hallways were lined with photos of smiling babies who had been conceived thanks to the hard work and skill of these doctors, nurses, lab technicians, and embryologists. Babies who went home with parents who had probably had just as little hope—and just as much fear—as I had.

My husband and I had blood tests and underwent several other routine exams. The results were not conclusive, but they did help us develop a plan.

It turned out that we were both contributing to the situation. Technically, they diagnosed us with "unexplained infertility." My husband's sperm count was fine, but the motility was slightly low. I had diminished ovarian reserve—fewer eggs than most women my age, which could contribute to ovulation issues.

Our doctor was not overly concerned about either individual result. The combination could create an issue, but he still felt we were good candidates for intrauterine insemination (IUI) before anything more invasive or expensive.

First, though, I would undergo a hysterosalpingogram (HSG) to make sure the issue was not a blocked fallopian tube.

Sometimes, my doctor said, the flushing of the tubes during the HSG removes a blockage and the issue is resolved.

No such luck. I thankfully had no tubal blockages, but even with the addition of a follicle-stimulating hormone drug (Letrozole), I still was not pregnant the next month.

It was time to try insemination.

You know how on television they just stick a turkey baster up there and magically the woman is inseminated? It doesn't work quite like that. IUI requires timing, vaginal ultrasounds, blood tests, specimen collection...oh, and waiting. Additionally, the fear that none of this was going to work was omnipresent. They don't show those parts on TV.

We had to give IUI our best try three times before moving on to something else (the scary acronym that took my breath away: IVF). Everyone at the fertility clinic was extremely optimistic.

Unfortunately, as the nurse explained (after the first month's vaginal ultrasound showing—oops—that I had ovulated earlier than they thought I would), the treatment could end up being merely a diagnostic tool. After leaving the clinic feeling disheartened that it would be yet another month until we could try IUI again, I started researching online. I asked Google, "What would make me ovulate early?"

I found many potential reasons to be unhelpful, including awful diseases that led me to believe one possibility was I was dying. One possibility that caught my attention was a short luteal phase. Most women have a 28-day cycle, but according to my app, my cycle was more like 24 to 26. This would explain why ovulation came earlier; the articles explained that it could also be a cause of not getting pregnant.

When I called my nurse to tell her I had gotten my period and was ready to start planning for IUI again, she had preemptively moved up the first scan by a day. So, I didn't mention my research. Obviously, these people knew what they were doing.

Two weeks later, I had my first ultrasound. My follicles were not yet large enough to release an egg. I had to come back the next day, and then the next. Finally, my follicles seemed large enough to release an egg, so I returned the following morning after my husband had dropped off his specimen. As I walked into the office and waved at the receptionist for the fourth day in a row, I realized I had become that woman I was so struck by at my first appointment. And I was only just about to complete my first (unsuccessful) IUI.

It ended up taking seven months to complete three unsuccessful attempts at IUI—seven months of waiting as time passed more slowly than I thought was possible, seven months of staring at exam-room ceilings hoping it would finally work this time; maybe this would be the last hospital ceiling I'd stare at until I was in a delivery room.

The difficulty we had in completing the three IUIs was partly attributable to what doctors eventually identified as my short, inconsistent luteal phase. And my diminished ovarian reserve likely played a role in my IUIs being unsuccessful and difficult to time. During the third month, I didn't even develop a single follicle that was mature enough to be released in ovulation. No wonder I hadn't been able to get pregnant the natural way; my ovaries were releasing immature eggs at random times. We didn't have a chance.

When I got my period after the third and final IUI, I was crushed. How would this ever work if I couldn't produce follicles (even with the help of Letrozole) and release them at a time when my husband's sperm could fertilize them?

And Then There Were None

It was time for in vitro fertilization (IVF).

The only reference I had for IVF was in one of my favorite episodes of *Friends*. In "The One with the Embryos," Phoebe is implanted with five embryos from her brother and sister-in-law. She goes to the doctor and talks to the embryos while wearing a hospital gown. Later in the day, she has a positive pregnancy test. I knew that couldn't be all there was to IVF, but boy, I had no idea.

At the clinic's two-hour IVF orientation session, we learned how to mix, draw up, and administer several types of shots. My husband learned how to give me "trigger shots" in the butt, and we read through instructions, dates, and plans. The IVF coordinator went through the process for egg retrieval and the subsequent embryo lab process. We had to decide whether we wanted to freeze our eggs. Did we want to genetically test them and find out about any abnormalities, or even the gender? Did we want to try for a "fresh transfer" (shortly after the egg retrieval as opposed to freezing the embryos and transferring them later)? Our doctor didn't recommend a fresh transfer, she explained, since genetic testing guaranteed better quality embryos, and he *never* implanted more than one embryo. *Never.*

I was overwhelmed. What had we gotten ourselves into, and why did we have to do this? Worse, we had to wait nearly six weeks to start our first round of IVF because we needed to work out financing the ridiculous cost (with zero help from insurance), order all the medicines and shots, and, oh right, wait for my menstrual cycle to begin again.

In addition to my impatience and paralyzing fear, I added another emotion to the mix: grief. I was grieving the loss of getting to conceive naturally, without conception having to be a scientific process involving embryologists in lab coats. Never would I get to enjoy the surprise of a positive pregnancy test in a bathroom like women did in commercials. I grieved the loss of the fun, intimate side of sex. The romance evaporates when your husband has to deposit his specimen in a cup once a month.

I also grieved the lack of teamwork in conceiving. I was the one who had to take the pills, keep track of the calendar, give myself shots, go in for blood tests and ultrasounds, and do everything else that went into IVF, all while still working full time. It was a lonely process, even with a supportive husband.

When the giant box from the fertility pharmacy arrived on our doorstep, I carefully unpacked each item and created a mini pharmacy on our dining room table, which became my mixing station, as well as the location for giving myself shots and checking off tasks. I organized the vials, syringes, needles, and pills, keeping in mind that this was thousands of dollars' worth of items displayed in front of me. The ultrasounds, blood tests, and egg retrieval procedure were beyond expensive, but I had had no idea how much the medicines would cost. The trigger shot alone cost almost as much as our monthly house payment.

After multiple days of ultrasounds, we finally saw clusters of follicles developing, which would eventually become large enough that I could take the ovulation trigger shot. Already I could tell that the number of follicles wasn't as high as is optimal, but it was a much better situation than we experienced with the IUIs.

After following weeks of directions to a tee, I underwent the egg retrieval procedure. I looked up at that hospital ceiling yet another time, tried to push back my fear and anxiety, and counted down as they told me to, aware of people and bright lights around me.

Somehow I drifted off, and what felt like seconds later I was in a recovery bed. The doctor explained that he had been able to retrieve six eggs and they had been sent to the lab. I should expect a call early the next morning to inform me of how many embryos had been successfully fertilized.

My voice caught in my throat. "Only six?"

He shook his head and left quietly.

After all that, I had only grown six mature follicles worth retrieving. I was heartbroken. Trying to reassure both of us that we hadn't just wasted thousands of dollars and another six weeks. My optimistic husband kept saying, "We only need one."

Just before 6 a.m. the next day, my phone buzzed. The embryologist said we had three fertilized eggs that they would monitor for development.

"Only three?" I asked, still half asleep.

She repeated the number and explained that she would call again in four days to let us know how many had made it that far and were ready to be frozen and tested.

I hung up and shook my head in disbelief. Six was bad enough, but now three?

Then came the call on a snowy winter morning, bringing us the news that our IVF cycle had been unsuccessful, resulting in zero embryos.

Round Two

My immediate thought was that we were finished trying. We couldn't afford to try again. I couldn't go through this again to get the same result. I was grieving the loss of those fertilized eggs that never even made it to embryos. I concluded that I would never be a mom, at least not this way.

Our doctor didn't know why the IVF round hadn't worked and wasn't sure whether repeating the process could yield different results. However, the reproductive endocrinologist shared his plan for a subsequent IVF procedure. He suggested a few tweaks to the protocol, including adding human growth hormone shots and using a different ovulation suppressant that might encourage more follicle growth.

My husband ate up every word; from the moment we had heard that it hadn't worked, he'd asserted that we would try again and it would work.

I, on the other hand, had little interest in another round of IVF. I needed something with a better chance of success. Just as when IUI had failed the first time, I started researching everything I could find about other options, including adoption, donated eggs, donated embryos, and experimental treatments. I wanted to do whatever would give us the best chance of getting a baby. I took time to navigate through my emotions and my thoughts. My family and husband were very supportive, but I needed to talk to someone who had gone through the same thing. I sought out a large infertility support group on Facebook and even attended the group's annual conference. I read several highly-rated books about infertility. I made an appointment with a therapist who had also gone through IVF. We met several times, both individually and with my husband, to help us try to decide our next step.

I also reached out to a high school friend I'd mostly lost touch with, but who had recently posted on Facebook about her infertility journey. She initially struggled with IVF but succeeded in the second cycle. I emailed her asking for any insight on how she and her husband had decided to try again and what they did differently to achieve success.

I never could have imagined the amazing reply that arrived in my inbox in less than 24 hours. She inspired me to do whatever I felt was right. She explained the lifestyle changes she and her husband had made, told me about books she had read, recommended nutritional supplements, gave me advice about acupuncture, and, most importantly, asserted that she knew I would become a mother one day if I wanted. She wasn't sure how exactly it would happen, but she knew in her heart that it would. Her words made me believe what my family and close friends had been telling me for months; sometimes it takes someone on the outside telling you something in order for you to really hear it.

I started to come around to the idea of trying IVF again, and my husband and I met with our therapist one more time. He explained why he was so interested in trying again, even though I was overcome with fear. "I'm a risk-reward guy," he said. "It's definitely the biggest risk, but it also has the biggest potential reward. A baby that is ours genetically would be the ultimate reward, and I'm willing to take an enormous risk for that."

These words from my husband melted my heart. He may have used a financial metaphor, but he was being vulnerable and honest. I knew then that we did need to try IVF again, in a slightly different way. I was going to do everything my friend had recommended for several months to make sure it would affect our potential success.

We did it all: took vitamins and supplements, abstained from caffeine and alcohol, exercised, and increased our fruit and vegetable consumption. I had 10 weeks of fertility treatment with a wonderful acupuncturist who focused on stimulating my ovaries with needle placement. Lying in her quiet office made me feel calm, and I figured it couldn't hurt to open my mind to an alternative type of healing that might help us get a baby.

My doctor implemented his new plan. He also had a backup plan that we hadn't been ready for during the first round: if the embryos were not good enough to freeze on day five but were still developing, we would do a fresh transfer that day. My husband would give me progesterone shots following egg retrieval to prepare my uterus for this possibility.

I would be 34 that summer, and I knew my time was running out. I was giving it my all while feeling terrified that none of it would work.

New Beginnings

I was now giving myself 10 shots per day. I have no idea how I did that. I could feel myself float up out of my body, pretending I was giving these shots to someone else. I also kept my eye on the prize and tried to remember my husband's words.

My second egg retrieval procedure was similar to the first time. It gave me a disturbing sense of déjà vu. This wasn't supposed to be a repeat; this time, I kept telling myself, would be different. One thing was not the same: the doctor held my hand and said a few encouraging words.

This time when I woke up from the egg retrieval, my mom told me they had gotten 13 eggs. Still nothing like what I had hoped, but it was more than double the amount from the first time. I did my best to stay positive.

This time we had eight eggs that had fertilized to create eight embryos. Again, I wasn't thrilled, but I reminded myself that this was a marked improvement. And, again, my husband said, "We only need one."

Five days later, I received the 6:08 a.m. morning phone call. I reluctantly slid my finger across the screen to answer the call, dreading what I would hear after "Hello."

I waited as that feeling of déjà vu crept over me a second time.

Her voice sounded a little different; she had good news and bad news. I braced myself and wasn't sure how it could be both—either we had an embryo or we didn't. The embryologist reported that two embryos had made it to day five and the blastocyst stage. Two! The bad news: neither was high enough quality to freeze and test for later implantation.

This meant we were moving on to Plan B; I would go in for a fresh transfer. We were doing this...today! I could barely comprehend what was about to happen. I sped to the hospital and met my husband out front. Neither of us could talk due to being so nervous, so we just held hands as we walked in together, going to a room in the clinic we had never been to during our many visits. It was the transfer "suite," and my doctor was there and ready.

The embryologist I'd spoken to that morning came in pushing a steel cart containing petri dishes. Months before I had loathed her for the news she'd delivered, but today she was back in my good graces. She showed us a printout of the magnified blastocysts, pointing out the irregularities and explaining how the quality was not high enough for them to be frozen. Accordingly, they would transfer both embryos and hope that one would stick.

This stopped me in my tracks. The IVF coordinator had told us several times that our doctor never transferred more than one embryo. Suddenly my optimism evaporated. Clearly, the doctor didn't think we had a chance with these low-quality embryos, so transferring both was a last resort. Once again, I found myself staring at the ceiling, waiting for the ultrasound and transfer, full of fear.

They sent me home with instructions to rest, continue nightly progesterone shots, and come back in nine days for a blood pregnancy test. I tried to keep busy with end-of-the-school-year tasks as the days slowly went by. I suddenly realized that I only had enough progesterone for eight days. I called the nurse in a panic and she explained that I would need to buy more and that it only came in larger quantities, which I might not end up needing, depending on the test results. I didn't want to risk missing one dose and gladly paid the $300 for a single vial, hoping it would do the trick.

Finally, the day of my pregnancy test arrived. I went in early and headed to work to wait for the call with the results. I figured it would be later in the day, yet at 10 a.m. I was startled by my phone buzzing. My favorite nurse was on the other end of the line.

"Well, it's a good thing you got that extra progesterone," she giggled.

"It worked?" I asked.

She said, "You're pregnant!"

Tears flooded my eyes. I had been waiting for such a long time to hear those words.

I called my husband, who was just as excited. "You're really pregnant!" he said.

The nurse had told me to keep taking the progesterone shots at night and to come in again in a few days to make sure my hormone levels kept rising appropriately. I repeated the tests a few days later, and again, my levels went up.

Even with all this good news, I wouldn't let myself get my hopes up. I had never been pregnant and wondered whether my body could stay pregnant. I had an ultrasound at six weeks and we saw the baby (only one—somehow one of those low-quality blastocysts had held on). I had another ultrasound at eight weeks and we saw the heartbeat and growth. We had made it to eight weeks: time to switch over to my regular OBGYN.

I couldn't believe this was happening. I had spent so much time at the clinic that I knew every nurse, the bookkeeper, the check-out clerk, the receptionists, the lab technicians, and the embryologist. I knew the best times to arrive for blood draws and what chairs were most comfortable in the waiting room. I knew the exact position to put myself in for a vaginal ultrasound. I even knew about the special suite for embryo transfer. But it was time to say goodbye.

Despite the progressing pregnancy, my impatience returned with a fury. I couldn't wait for being pregnant to be over so that I could finally be a mother. I also grappled with the fear that at any minute, the pregnancy could end and we would be back at square one.

In month eight, after my baby shower, my sister observed that I hadn't set up the nursery and items still had the tags on. She started to take off the tags, and I nearly had a panic attack. I realized I was still paralyzed with fear that this baby would not survive and I would have to return everything. Fortunately, I had her to help me through that, but that fear didn't leave until I held my baby boy in my arms at age 34 1/2, more than five years after deciding to try for a family.

As my fear started to subside, guilt settled in its place. I felt guilty because I continued to delay my long-awaited pregnancy announcement due to paralyzing fear of a miscarriage; I felt guilty that my husband had basically had to force me to try IVF again, and that I was adamant that it wouldn't work; and, more than anything, I felt guilty that it *had* worked—it doesn't for everyone.

Through the years, I had come to know many people experiencing similar battles with infertility. I learned of even more when I finally did post a pregnancy announcement (but acknowledged how difficult it had been for us and the empathy we felt for those still going through their journeys). While it had taken us years to achieve success, others had spent even more time and even more money, with no success. What had I done to deserve this miracle?

More Waiting and Wondering

Even now, as my son is about to turn two, I impatiently wait for each workday to end so I can be with him.

I still feel guilty because IVF worked for us and not others, and I also feel the ubiquitous "mom guilt" when I take a moment for myself. I worked so hard to get this kid; I shouldn't leave him in daycare a minute longer than necessary, I shouldn't get a babysitter for a night out, I shouldn't look at Facebook for even a minute as he plays in front of me.

I also feel intense guilt about not being able to do IVF again. I'm terrified my son will despise being an only child. Was it selfish of us to do so much to get this one child and then deny him siblings? Maybe.

But even if I wanted to, or we had the money, I wouldn't go through IVF again. We got a miracle baby out of a "Plan B low-quality embryo" fresh transfer that I'm pretty sure my doctor didn't think would work. I don't see us getting that lucky again.

And now that I'm 36, I don't have time on my side.

I don't have all night to wait for a call to light up my phone when I have to get up with a toddler at 7 a.m.

I don't have days to rest in bed after an egg retrieval procedure when I spend my days playing with cars and blowing bubbles.

I don't have months to spend researching options, getting acupuncture, taking vitamins, and going to therapy when those months would be better spent witnessing incredible changes in a growing child.

And I certainly don't have five more years to turn our family of three into a family of four.

What I do have is a bright, beautiful boy who lights up my life and has given me the greatest gift I could have imagined. My road to motherhood was winding and long, but I made it here. It took a supportive family, helpful friends, way too much money, and more strength than I thought I had—plus an immeasurable amount of waiting, fear, grief, and, eventually, guilt—but it was worth it.

He is worth it. ■

MEGAN PALMER lives in Overland Park, Kansas, with her husband and son, who was born in early 2019. She teaches high-school journalism in Kansas City and has written for several magazines and other publications over the years. You can contact her at meganpalmer731@gmail.com or follow her on Instagram @meganpalmer731.

Second Chances

HANNAH ROBERTSON

The first time I was pregnant was in the fall of 2008. I had just celebrated my first wedding anniversary with my then-husband and I was on cloud nine about expecting our first child (and the first grandchild on either side of the family). I had become pregnant after only a couple of months of trying, and other than a little nausea, I felt great.

We announced the pregnancy on my birthday (and that of my husband's grandfather). We sent grandparent cards and gifted framed sonogram photos. The news was received with the tears, excitement, and love one would expect. We treasured having the chance to tell all of our family in one place that we were going to be having a baby the following spring, and we videotaped it.

I saw my doctor once a month for the first few months, and all appeared normal. As nausea and discomfort started ramping up, I was feeling thankful to be pregnant with a healthy baby. I believed that the physical symptoms meant the pregnancy was progressing.

Something Was Wrong

Then, in November 2008, on a Friday, I felt a little off. I was 16 weeks pregnant. I called my OBGYN and the office staff told me that it was early pregnancy discomfort and not to worry too much, but to let them know on Monday if things were the same. On Monday, I had some cramping and felt like something was wrong. A week earlier, the baby had had a strong heartbeat and my blood work had been normal; no one was worried about these symptoms, but the doctor asked me to come in to make sure everything was OK.

As I drove to the appointment, I was hit by the sudden, unmistakable feeling that things were *not* OK. The sun was incredibly bright. It was crisp and cold and pretty outside, especially in the middle of November. Yet as I drove, the fear that something was wrong continued to build.

I arrived at the doctor's office and was ushered into an exam room. The nurse used a doppler to try to find a heartbeat for a few minutes. When she could not find one, I was moved to a consultation room and told to wait for an ultrasound technician. The staff tried to assure me that the baby was just hiding and an ultrasound would confirm that all was well. But I knew. I knew all was most definitely *not* well. I called my husband and asked him to meet me at the doctor's office. While he was making the drive, I sat alone and slowly started to unravel in the tiny, windowless room.

When my husband arrived, I was taken to an ultrasound room where the technician immediately confirmed there was no heartbeat, when there had been one just a week earlier. Our baby had died at about 14 weeks gestation. I remember the technician explaining that the baby was about the size of my hand. After that, I just shut down for the rest of the explanation.

Devastated is not a strong enough word for how I felt at that moment. The news was soul-crushing. I instantly felt ashamed and guilty, as if I had done something wrong to cause our baby to die.

We were taken to another exam room to meet with the doctor and discuss the next steps.

When the doctor came in, he explained that I could either deliver the baby or we could schedule a dilation and curettage (D&C). I chose to deliver because I wanted to bring our baby into the world myself.

We went upstairs to the Labor and Delivery floor to start the process. The delivery was brutal. There are large parts of that night that I do not remember. I do vividly remember the moment my son was born. I will always remember: 1:17 a.m. on November 18, 2008. I could sense how tiny he was. I was asked if I wanted to see him, and I said no. I wanted to remember my baby as I had imagined him in my mind: perfect, having my nose and his dad's hair. I signed the paperwork for the funeral home to take him and zoned out for the next 12 hours.

I was discharged the next day and given instructions on how to care for myself (physically). I had a follow-up appointment scheduled with my OBGYN for the next week. I left the hospital feeling numb and destroyed, all at the same time. We had to stop at the store on the way home to make sure I had everything I needed as I recovered. That was the most surreal experience of the day. I remember standing in the store, trying to decide what kind of pads I should purchase, not fully comprehending what I needed or how this situation had even transpired. When we got home, my husband force-fed me vegetable soup and covered me with blankets while I sat lifelessly on the couch.

The home health nurse checked on me three days later. The nurse confirmed that I was healing well, and she left. I fell apart again. I felt so lost. And alone. My mom, who is my best friend, was there; however, she had had two healthy pregnancies and two healthy babies. This was new territory for her, too.

We were fortunate to find out that our baby boy had had Trisomy 18 (Edwards Syndrome). This chromosomal abnormality is not compatible with life, and even if I had been able to carry him to term, he would not have lived long after he was born. We learned that there was a chance I was a carrier for the genetic issue. Yet after extensive genetic testing, it was determined that I was not. Therefore, our son's diagnosis of Edwards Syndrome was the result of an unlikely chance occurrence that caused him to have an extra 18th chromosome. Obtaining this knowledge eased my mind: I could try to have another baby and the chances of this happening again would be very low. Yet the knowledge also caused my guilt and self-blame to increase, as I believed it was my body that had failed our baby.

Anxious and Alone

As the weeks passed, I struggled to get my feet back under me. My husband began to spend more time away from me. I'm sure it was painful for him to watch me suffer. It was likely easier for him to not see me and be able to pretend the miscarriage and subsequent pain were not happening. I was starting to struggle with crippling anxiety and depression. And I was even experiencing full-blown panic attacks that required visits to the emergency room. I was terrified to be by myself. But I was also terrified to be around people for fear that I would have a panic attack in front of someone and make them uncomfortable. And I would eat only two or three foods because I was terrified that something I ate was going to cause a panic attack.

One day during the height of my depression and anxiety, I was talking to my mom on the phone. I was crying, and she reminded me that the home health nurse had said that if someone close to me told me they felt like something was wrong, I needed to listen to them. My mom gently mentioned that I was not OK and it probably wouldn't hurt for me to talk to a professional about my emotional and mental state. I reluctantly agreed to see a therapist.

My mental health had been rapidly deteriorating due to dealing with the loss of my son and having to process the loss without a supportive spouse. My physical health was rapidly declining because of the stress of losing the baby and trying to keep my marriage together. During the next year and a half, I was in and out of my doctor's and therapist's offices, as well as the emergency room, trying to figure out how to return to some sense of normalcy.

The state of my marriage continued to worsen. With hindsight, I can now see that my then-husband and I were undoubtedly processing the loss in vastly different ways. We viewed the loss from different vantage points and we couldn't understand the other's perspective. We were at different stages of the grieving process. And these differences drove us further apart. Fortunately, I was still able to make progress in healing myself. I had been forced to say goodbye to my baby. The pain associated with that is not something that ever goes away, but

I was blessed to have people in my life who helped me navigate my way back to a more normal existence in which I could function.

Even after receiving professional help to work through the trauma of losing our son, I still struggled with panic, anxiety, and lingering mental health issues. I was making strides, though, even if only in incremental steps. Unfortunately, my husband was not willing to hang onto our marriage any longer, and our union ultimately did not survive. After two-and-a-half years of marriage and many years together, we divorced.

I had now failed at attaining the role of mother as well as that of wife. This was a very difficult time. As a Type A over-achiever, I wanted to change the fact that I had lost a baby and a marriage, and the fact that I couldn't was difficult to accept.

Starting Over

I did, however, start to recognize that I now had the freedom to take care of myself—just myself—and do what I needed to do to keep getting better. I focused on therapy and other forms of self-care, such as routine exercise. And I redirected a lot of my energy toward my professional life. These activities helped me move my life in a positive direction. I slowly started to realize that I hadn't failed at anything and had instead embarked on a path of critical self-discovery.

About a year and a half after separating from my husband, I was set up on a blind date with the neighbor of a woman I had met while teaching summer school. When the day came for the date, I was at my parents' house and not looking forward to going; I was complaining to my mom about having to go back to my apartment and shower and get cleaned up to go on a date with the neighbor of someone I barely knew. It seemed like a giant waste of time. Luckily, I went anyway.

I met my current husband, Chris, at a restaurant on Sunday, June 5, 2011. We left three hours later, having talked about seemingly every possible topic. We met for drinks on Monday, went for a motorcycle ride on Tuesday, and introduced our dogs to each other on Wednesday. We got engaged on September 5 and married on December 30. Yes, all in 2011! He is truly my happily ever after. He is my second chance that I never knew I wanted or needed. He loves me unconditionally and in spite of—or perhaps because of—all of my quirks and struggles.

The spring after we got married, we decided to try to get pregnant. I was terrified and still trying to fully process the trauma of my first pregnancy. Part of me knew, though, that to process the loss of my son completely, I would need to have faith and try again. I was cautiously optimistic.

I got pregnant within a couple of months. I spent the early months physically sick and afraid that something was going to go wrong at any moment.

My initial checkups went well and confirmed that I was carrying a healthy baby. I still struggled with accepting this information because I had been told that same thing before, and it had ultimately proved to be wrong. As time passed and everything continued to go well, I tried to relax and enjoy being pregnant.

At 19 weeks, I started to have issues associated with preterm labor. Preterm labor symptoms remained throughout my pregnancy. I spent an exorbitant amount of time at my doctor's office and in the Labor and Delivery department taking medicine to stop contractions. I was instructed to limit my activity severely and sit or lie down as much as possible.

At my 20-week appointment, we found out that we were having a baby boy. However, we also found out that he had some cysts in his brain. This happens frequently without issue, but it can be a marker for Edwards Syndrome. We were going to have to wait a month and a half to see a specialist to confirm that the cysts were benign, and he had no genetic issues.

Shortly after learning of the possibility that my second son might also have Edwards Syndrome, I learned that I also had gestational diabetes. While working through the preterm labor and the cysts concern, this added diagnosis was a lot to handle. Fortunately, gestational diabetes is manageable. Chris and I set out to learn and do everything we could to keep the baby and me healthy through the rest of my pregnancy.

My anxiety skyrocketed as the appointment to see the specialist about the cysts approached. On the day of the appointment, I was a wreck. I went to the restroom beforehand. I got on my knees and asked God to watch over us and let our baby be healthy. I was in tears and so scared. As I settled onto the table for the detailed ultrasound, I continued to pray that he was OK. After an hour of checking out every single part of his little body, the technician confirmed that he was indeed a very healthy little boy.

My sole focus thereafter became keeping him inside me for as long as possible.

In March 2013, after lots of rest and trying to stay calm, and then an entire day of labor, I delivered him. He was healthy, huge, and hungry!

In a serendipitous turn of events, the same doctor who delivered my first son under terrible circumstances delivered this healthy baby boy. It was reassuring to know that my journey to having a healthy baby had come full circle.

Over the next several years, my husband and I enjoyed raising our son and also took time to focus on our careers. After a couple of cross-country moves and building a new house, we were ready to try for a second child. We'd known we wanted to have two children, and we finally felt ready to add to our family.

After just a few months of trying, in the spring of 2017, we learned that I was again pregnant. We were elated to give our oldest son a sibling. I had blood work done, and all looked like it was going well.

Yet at my eight-week appointment, we learned that there was, in fact, no baby. I was diagnosed with a blighted ovum and scheduled for a D&C the next day. It was mentally difficult not to go straight back to my first pregnancy or wallow in the same emotions I had felt with my first loss: guilt, shame, and a sense of failure.

This time, though, I had a husband who stepped up. He took care of our son so I could rest and spend time speaking to my therapist to avoid having my anxiety completely spiral out of control again. We took several months to regroup and started trying again in the late summer.

We learned we were again pregnant in August 2017. And again, I felt afraid and doubtful. Fortunately, I had a robust support system and I was able to take it a day at a time and appreciate every day that I was nauseated and pregnant.

It was difficult deciding when to tell our older son about the pregnancy. A part of me wanted to wait as long as possible in case something happened. We ultimately decided at the three-month mark to tell him the news so he could be involved in the process of becoming a big brother.

This pregnancy progressed smoothly, with no issues other than one round of heavy contractions, which my doctor was able to stop with medication. As the baby's due date neared, I was able to relax and truly enjoy being pregnant. I know this is not often the case for a lot of people who have suffered through a loss, and I feel blessed that I had those few months when I could revel in the experience of growing a tiny human inside my body.

Our second son came into the world after a flurry of contractions and a quick drive to the hospital; we arrived with about an hour to spare. I got to pull my healthy baby out of my body with my own two hands. It was a remarkable experience and a special way to welcome our son into this world.

I thank God every day for my second chance. My second chance to be a wife to an amazing husband. My second chance to carry sweet little humans in my body. My second chance to be a mama in the traditional sense of the word—that is, to hold my babies in my arms.

I do still struggle with panic attacks and anxiety. I have made headway in learning how to live my everyday life with the underlying current of past trauma and experiences. And while those experiences will never disappear, and my losses will always be a part of my story, my pregnancy losses are no longer my entire story. Do I have days when I'm bitter and frustrated, or sometimes just plain sad? Absolutely. Yet those tough days have grown fewer and further between. For that, I am extremely grateful. I've chosen to frame my past loss as protection; protection from a life and a relationship that may not have been the best for helping me thrive.

Today I have two very happy little boys, ages eight and three, and a husband who is my rock. I am keenly aware that without the struggle and hardship I endured, I would not be where I am today. I feel extremely fortunate to be a mama to my boys. I know my story has a traditionally happy ending, while lots of similar stories do not yet have one. I would implore you to hang on. Sometimes the best things come from second chances. ■

HANNAH ROBERTSON lives in Des Moines, Iowa, with her husband and two sons. Hannah teaches English to Chinese students online and owns her own business. When she has a free moment, Hannah loves to read, watch obscure documentaries about topics nobody has ever heard of, and spend time with her family every chance she gets. You can contact Hannah at hannah.k.robertson@gmail.com.

You Were Meant for Me

SHERI STURNIOLO

"Your ovaries are deaf," said the doctor.

"Dead? My ovaries are dead?"

"No," she corrected me, "Your ovaries are *deaf.*"

That was basically the *Oh crap* moment when I knew my road to motherhood was going to be less like a run to the grocery store and more like a cross-country manhunt with no GPS. This was one of the first visits with my reproductive endocrinologist. My husband and I had decided that we would pull out the big guns and "go for the gold," or more accurately, for the "golden eggs."

With several thousand dollars, I happily purchased the best hormones and ovarian stimulants money could buy. I had high hopes that this magical potion would seduce my old ovaries into an interpretive dance of fertility. Before they knew what was happening, pop! Out would come an egg!

The dance was less like a tango and more like a 6th-grade winter formal.

The Beginning of the Journey

But let me back up a bit. This moment, while momentous, was not the beginning of my journey to motherhood. It was one of many moments that got me to where I am today: mother to two of the sweetest babes born to me through embryo donation. Spoiler alert: my path was hard, my tears were many, and my world was turned upside down, but there was much enlightenment in my struggle. Infertility is indeed one of the most heartbreaking and core-shattering challenges a woman can endure. In all of that adversity, however, there is an equally powerful gift of transformation. Like a caterpillar to a butterfly, or sand to a pearl; there is beauty formed from the transformational elements of pressure, patience, and perseverance. Whatever analogy you can relate to, just try your darndest not to be the thorny weed that grows in that crack on the highway. Yes, that thorny weed is resilient, but it is lonely and pokey.

I, like many young women in their twenties, found myself having a grand old time traveling the world and enjoying all that life had to offer. I had a plan: travel, meet the man of my dreams, and then have children. And if that did not work, plan B was to have children anyway, even without a husband. I figured age 35 would be a good time to pull the emergency switch on my biological clock.

When I was 30, I did, in fact, meet Mr. Wonderful. We did the obligatory dating time, the obligatory married time, and ended up trying to conceive when I was 35. Perfect timing, right? Wrong. After one year of trying and my first of three miscarriages heavy on my heart, we went looking for answers.

The answer we found was that time had been up some time ago. My ovarian reserve was nonexistent, and my ovaries laughed a wicked laugh at my body's inferior monthly hormone delivery. My reproductive endocrinologist told me from day one that we could *try* with my own eggs, but more than likely I would need to use donor eggs given that my ovaries "were deaf."

On the Road Again

Fast forward through three more years of fertility treatments. We were broke and broken. Once again, we were staring at our doctor, having the same conversation about donor conception that we had had at the beginning of our infertility journey. There was a difference this time, though. The path I'd walked took me somewhere I didn't think I'd arrive. It took me to a place of clarity and acceptance.

My "transformation" was not a pretty one (think less caterpillar to butterfly and more gremlin meets water). As my doctor had predicted, I never made enough eggs to justify the risk and expense of an in vitro fertilization (IVF) cycle using my own eggs. This realization led to an unsightly, albeit necessary, phase of grieving. I screamed, I cried, and I threw things. I felt resentment toward anyone who got pregnant. I felt left behind and left out of the motherhood club to which I had surely been promised membership. I felt angry. And then, slowly, a deep sadness engulfed me. I listened to emotionally cathartic music while staring out at the nothingness. *Summertime Sadness* and *Young & Beautiful* by Lana Del Rey played on repeat, and I allowed myself to wallow.

I was shocked and in emotional turmoil while at the same time emotionally numb. The emptiness felt overwhelming. After bathing in self-pity for what seemed like an appropriate amount of time and absorbing all the sadness I could manage,

I got mad again. Not mad like I had before, though. Tenacity kicked back in and my response was, "No way am I going to let this disable me." For most of my adult life, I had felt like a hostage to my emotions, struggling to identify, process, address, and analyze my feelings adequately. I knew that allowing myself to acknowledge my feelings of loss, sadness, and anger, and to process them in my own way on my own timeline, was crucial. It was imperative that I work through these big emotions, especially around something as significant as motherhood. Having something like your fertility seemingly stolen is hard, but stealing something from *myself* felt worse. That something was my own happiness. So, I turned off the melancholy playlist and got back *On the Road Again*.

Hitting A Dead End and Finding a New Path

After four intrauterine inseminations (IUIs) and two more miscarriages (one stemming from the IUIs and the other from a natural conception), my husband and I tried IVF using donor eggs. With a newfound sense of hope and excitement, I flipped through the files of egg donors. It was both bizarre and surreal. I mean, who were these women? Why were they donating their precious eggs? What were their hopes and dreams of becoming mothers themselves one day? Oddly, I felt a sense of both connection and unfamiliarity. The egg donor program in the United States was, at that time, mostly anonymous, meaning that after a woman donated there was no relationship between the parties and no connection besides the genetic one between the donor and baby. One of these women would play one of the most important roles in my life, yet I would only know her through a profile.

I tried to envision the women in the profiles creating a child with my husband (a very peculiar thought) and imagine what the child would look like. I scanned hundreds of women's profiles, studying their every image and dissecting their responses to the questions they had been asked by the donor agency. I was searching for a sign from the universe that she was *the one.*

Given that donor egg IVF cycles are so costly, I felt this was our one chance. We had been given the option to take part in a "split cycle" (half the eggs, half the cost) with another couple at the clinic but had passed. We wanted to have the best chance we could, and for that, we needed all the eggs we could get. Or so we thought. It's funny that at that moment, when offered that option, I had no idea what the universe had in store for me.

Back to the excitement! Imagine the exhilaration when our donor had her egg retrieval (after going through IVF) and the retrieval yielded 26 beautifully bouncy eggs, 26 orbs of hope, 26 chances to meet our child. All but a done deal, right?

Not exactly. The next day, the embryologist called to report that *zero*, yes, *zero* of the 26 eggs had been fertilized using my husband's sperm.

I was driving to work and had pulled over to take the embryologist's call. Anyone who has taken the call from an embryologist after an IVF cycle knows what a nerve-wracking experience it is. But I was utterly unprepared for the cascade of devastation I would soon experience. I got off the phone in complete shock. I became intensely angry. Yes, I was in disbelief over the news, but all the other moments I had endured over the previous three years were very much present as well. The devastation rose in me like a wave and I screamed an ugly and visceral scream as my mind caught up and my heart dropped. The impact was so unbearable that all I could do was slam my fists into the steering wheel again and again and again. For hours, all I did was cry, shake my head, and scream.

This level of emotional trauma was a tipping point, and the trauma opened something in my heart and mind. That something was the beginning of acceptance. Specifically, acceptance of a path that was starting to reveal itself to me: a path to motherhood through embryo donation.

However, as this transformation was underway internally, outwardly my husband and I were maximizing that last glimpse of light that was struggling to shine through the closing door. While my heart was beginning to accept the possibility of embryo donation, we tried again with donor eggs. This detour took us to a split cycle with an unknown couple. While this route was a whole lot less expensive, and with fewer eggs retrieved, it would later prove to be one of the most valuable moments in our journey. This route ultimately helped yield the clarity I needed around my road to motherhood.

The Case of the Egg Assassin

I took yet another call from the embryologist after our second IVF cycle with donor eggs. One day after intracytoplasmic sperm injection (ICSI) was performed with the donor's eggs and my husband's sperm, the embryologist informed me that no eggs had been fertilized.

Yep, none.

Strangely, I was only moderately phased this time. My mind and heart had hardened from the experiences of the past.

The extremely important bit of information was that the other half of the eggs received by the other couple had been fertilized. How could that be? My husband's sperm had received a passing grade; not necessarily in the Michael Phelps club, but they had qualified in all the right trials. Also, to their credit, they had been successful three times prior fertilizing my old-lady eggs (twice through natural conception and once through IUI, although all three times ended in miscarriages). But with more than 40 hope-filled donor eggs a distant memory, my husband became a self-proclaimed egg assassin, and we moved on.

Next stop embryo donation, right? Not quite. Acting on this latest bit of intel about my husband's sperm was like feeling compelled to take an exit on a long road trip, despite being only blocks from your destination. There it was, that annoyingly calm "recalculating route." I could not leave this stone unturned. Maybe my eggs were old but not quite ready to ride off into the sunset. Maybe it was all my husband's fault. What if, what if, what if? Male infertility was a possible explanation for our struggles. This was about my husband now; replacing him in the equation. This felt different.

A Hopeful Journey: "Ticket for One; I Mean, 10 Million!"

We headed back to science for answers. Although none of my husband's fertility tests had indicated that there would be a problem on his end, we opted to dig deeper with another specialized semen analysis that looked at the fragmentation of the DNA his sperm carried.

I will never forget standing at the copy store's counter with my gigantic shiny silver cryopreservation tank. "Um, what is that?" asked the young fellow behind the counter. A valid question, I admit, yet I wasn't sure how to answer. I mean, was I obligated to report biological material? Would they try to open it like the airport security officers do and leave a little note inside saying they had inspected my vial of sperm? I looked at him with a somewhat guilty look and said "Sperm." He pursed his lips and muttered, "Hmmm, OK," and away the sperm went.

This new journey, this glimmer of hope like with any other fertility test, treatment, or home pregnancy test, was just another stop along our road. It was another small breath of oxygen keeping our hope alive, even if only for a little longer. I say that because, as clichéd as it sounds, the road that you travel, the stops that you make, the detours that you encounter—they all become *your journey*. And in turn, all the detours you take help you process, in your own way, the destination at which you arrive. Just as everyone is unique, each of our journeys will be unique. Each person will try different methods. What is acceptable to some women may not be acceptable to others. Some women have a deep yearning to carry their child. Some do not have a strong desire for carrying but long for a child who has their eyes and hands. Some are guided by their religious or spiritual beliefs that only allow certain types of fertility treatments, while others want a child to nurture and love, and feel that the way in which that child joins their family is not bound by genetics or pregnancy.

Allowing myself the time to take and explore all of those exits, detours, and dead ends was what ultimately gave me peace around, and acceptance of, how I would become a mother. I wasn't this all-knowing during my struggling years. I was more like a beginner pilot on my first transatlantic flight, with clear skies turning an ominous gray as I headed into a hurricane. The panels were shaking, bolts were threatening to dislodge, and my compass was no longer worth a damn. I had no option but to push every button and pull every lever, just hoping that something would work and I would land on solid ground. Every negative pregnancy test, every canceled fertility treatment, every fertility shot, every friend's baby shower almost had me calling "Mayday!" For me, the only thing worse than infertility was the thought of giving up. So, I kept going until I was looking into the eyes of my newborn son.

Back to the sperm on their journey. We waited anxiously for answers as to why none of the young and healthy donor eggs were being fertilized. Alas, nothing spectacular emerged from this somewhat comical detour. The sperm were healthy and their DNA fragments were not the issue. Still, something was amiss. How could I get pregnant three times naturally without high-tech intervention? I was not quite ready to submit to the diagnosis of unexplained infertility.

If Not You, My Dear, Then Who?

The next option was trying an IUI using donor sperm and my own eggs. Deciding whether to do this was not as easy a decision as the earlier decision to use donor eggs. I had resigned myself to the strong possibility that I would not be part of my child's genetics, but I had thought my husband would. I was OK taking on the role of the parent without a genetic connection, but this felt different.

We reluctantly went down the path of donor sperm, perusing sperm-bank profiles and looking for anything that felt right. This was yet another odd experience as we pondered how to choose the right profile. Should we focus on appearance, intellect, the donor's smile, or his favorite soda? Some profiles had baby pictures, and some had both baby and adult photos.

Let me just say that most all humans are cute at birth, but this does not always carry over to adulthood. There seemed to be too many options.

I found the profile of a donor who basically looked like my father-in-law had as a baby. A sign, I thought. It felt a bit like that game in which you spin the globe, close your eyes, and put your finger on it: wherever your finger lands is where you are destined to live.

We did not tell anyone about this path. We (and our family and close friends) had grown fatigued by all the ups and downs that had accompanied our infertility journey over the years, and I wasn't sure how others would respond to hearing that we were pursuing sperm donation. I had previously busted at the seams to discuss any and all details of our IUI and IVF cycles. Discussing sperm donation felt different. It felt taboo. As much as the words "infertility" and "women" seemingly go together, there appears to be more stigma attached to male infertility. Maybe it's because as women it is in our nature to share, discuss situations, and support each other. Men seem less inclined to divulge details about their private lives, let alone their infertility struggles. Now, I am in no way suggesting men are emotionless oafs who beat their chests and run around professing their virility, but there is a palpable difference when it comes to male infertility. I was keenly aware of this as we were exploring sperm donation. I never wanted my husband to feel that he was the problem or any less of a man, which is why I kept uncharacteristically quiet about our sperm donation cycle. Upon reflection, I believe I gave oxygen to the stigma of shame with my silence.

Nevertheless, we forged ahead with the sperm donor cycle, me assuming *the position* on the cold exam table, trying to get my body to relax while a plastic tube went in the "sperm-only door." There I was, once again, singing *Songs of My People* in my head, "Please, please, please let this work." There was an air of awkwardness in the room, as if a secret experiment was about to happen.

So, in went the donor sperm and out came my answer (10 days later, when the pregnancy test was yet again negative). I felt a sense of relief that it had not worked. During the two-week wait, I imagined what life would be like if I had had a child, genetically mine but not my husband's, and I didn't feel wonderful about it. I was ready to explain the lack of my blue eyes and blonde hair, ready to share the amazing story of conception via egg donation, but I felt uncertain about how I would navigate and explain the opposite situation.

I came to realize that if we could not conceive a child that included my husband, I'd rather that neither of us plays a genetic role. All of our trying, all of the treatments to attempt to include a genetic tie to one of us, were not that important to me anymore. Now in the beginning I had to work through the shock and emotional loss of having the expected genetic connection taken away, but I think the rest of our journey was for me to exhaust all the possibilities, working through all the "What if" and "Why me?" thoughts.

Our arduous road reminded me of my microbiology lab final. If you have not taken microbiology, let me walk you through the final exam. You get assigned a petri dish with some unknown organism growing in a gelatinous jar. To pass, you put the specimen through a series of biochemical tests, all of which you hope you've mastered during the course. With each of eight tests, you either identify or rule out the identity of your specimen. In my fertility journey, as it was with my microbiology final, it was as though I had been assigned the path that required all eight tests to reveal the specimen's identity. I can't help but laugh and wonder if maybe there is something to the saying, "You aren't given more than you can handle."

Together at Last

So, there we were, right where we were supposed to be. After our donor sperm cycle, we had one more naturally conceived pregnancy (that again resulted in a loss). We then decided to add our names to the fertility clinic's waitlist for embryo donation. Not only because it appeared to be our *only* path, but because it was *the* path. We had learned about embryo donation from our reproductive endocrinologist; before that, I had never heard of it. The prospect of being able to carry a baby was exhilarating for me. I could feel it: the universe was aligning, our orbit was steadying, our coordinates were set, and a little light in that vast darkness was heading our way.

After nearly six months on the waitlist, we received a call. A couple wanted to donate their frozen embryos to us! We were ecstatic. Our answer was a resonant "Yes! Yes! Yes!" We wanted those beautiful, frosty little babies.

There are many different ways that embryos are donated. The origin of each embryo and how it comes to be is unique. Some donated embryos are genetically tied to a couple, some are created using a donor's eggs and the husband's sperm, or vice versa, and some are created using both an egg donor and a sperm donor.

The embryos we received were donated by a couple who had used an egg donor. We were not able to know much about the sperm source, but we saw photos of the egg donor. This is when

I knew the universe had it all planned out. These embryos had been made using eggs from the very same egg donor we had been given the opportunity to use in a "split cycle" the previous year (but we had passed on that opportunity).

While my wish to experience pregnancy was graciously granted by the universe, in hindsight perhaps I should have specified that I wanted to experience an uneventful pregnancy. Alas, a few months into the pregnancy, I was diagnosed with vasa previa. It is similar to placenta previa but with a wicked twist: the baby's umbilical vessels are pretty much implanted on top of the "exit door." This means the internal end of the cervix, which the baby would otherwise pass through during birth, becomes a tangled mess of arteries and veins that provide the baby with life-sustaining nutrients and oxygen.

The problem is that you cannot simply wait for signs of labor and perform a cesarean section to bypass this vascular anomaly. The baby's vessels are pretty much attached to a fault line with an earthquake guaranteed to happen at any time. Even normal and otherwise benign contractions and cervical softening that occur in the final months of pregnancy can cause those fragile vessels to rupture. The probable outcome of this condition is a stillbirth.

At 25 weeks, I stood up and felt a gush of fluid, and my heart sank. As I was driven to the hospital, I leaned back in the passenger seat with my legs up in an attempt to protect any intact vessels from additional pressure; I wondered if this baby was going to stay with us.

In what seemed like a surreal combination of calm and chaos, the labor and delivery nurses hooked me up to the monitor, and we all listened for that rhythmic sound. And there it was, my son's heartbeat, strong and loud, tenacious and determined, indicative that despite a genetic connection, he had some of the same traits as his momma. We weren't out of the woods yet, but at that moment, all was well.

Locked Up

I was checked in for the remainder of the pregnancy (or at least until 34 weeks, when they would perform the required cesarean safely). I needed to be within minutes of the operating room in case a bleed should occur again. After the first 48 hours of multiple IV attempts, multiple medications to settle my uterus, and not being able to get up to go to the bathroom or drink anything, I cried. I could not fathom how I was to endure another 70 days of this. Any movement I made could take everything away. I was grateful to still be pregnant; I knew that other women who arrived with me that night were not so fortunate, and that outcome terrified me.

To understand how particularly difficult this strict bedrest with constant fetal monitoring was for me, you would need to talk to my mother. As a child, I despised not being able to move freely or even be bound by restrictive clothing.

I passed those two-plus months lying in bed watching *Keeping Up with the Kardashians* and *Fixer Upper* and waiting for Thursday, when pulled pork sandwiches were on the hospital menu. My husband was there night and day, only going home to sleep a couple of times a week when he had to work the next day; his strength and support no doubt kept us both healthy and hopeful.

Being a nurse myself, I know we can be very gracious, while also perhaps demanding, patients. I can imagine I was probably not everyone's favorite patient. The nurses, however, allowed me to give my own injections, schedule my medications and monitoring (as much as possible), and have a daily 15-minute wheelchair ride. This gave me some semblance of control over a very out-of-control situation. The first time my husband wheeled me down to the lobby and out into the cool night air, I could not do much except weep, overwhelmed by the crushing feeling of being imprisoned and briefly experiencing a moment of "freedom."

Go Time

After four years of trying to get pregnant, hundreds of shots, multiple miscarriages, and months of confinement, it was surreal to be rolling down the hall to the operating room on the day of my scheduled cesarean. As I lied on the operating table staring up at the ceiling while they prepped me, I tried with all my might to relax and keep my body calm. My husband sat beside me dressed in the "space suit" required for the operating room; all I could see were his eyes. I was so ready to see my son's face. The doctors pushed and pulled and just about lifted my body off of the surgery table. Hot tears rushed down my face as cheers filled the room. He was out! He was here! At that moment my world became forever more beautiful. I got a quick peek at his sweet little face before they took him to check him out. I heard his first cry. Our hearts both nearly burst at that moment. When they brought him to me, I kissed him softly and said, "I've been waiting for you."

I look back on this fleeting moment now and recognize how powerful it was. I feel so fortunate to have been given the opportunity to carry and nurture this precious being. On the day he was born my gratitude went out into the universe as

I thought of the generosity and love of those who chose to give him a chance at life and gave me a chance to be his mother.

You may be unsure about this particular road to motherhood and having a child with no genetic connection to you, as well as how the child may feel when he comes to understand his origins. I wish I could transmit all that I feel for my son, and now also his biological sister, into your heart. I would love to say that you will not worry about how and when to tell your child his unique creation story. I wish I could promise that he will never wonder what it means to have been born this way and never ask you hard questions about who those people are who helped bring him into the world. I cannot promise you that this path will be free of sacrifice or worry. What I can assure you is that there is no love greater than that between a mother and child, regardless of how the relationship came into being. When your child looks at you and sees nothing less than his entire world in your eyes, your heart will know that you are his mother and your road will forever lead to him. ■

SHERI STURNIOLO lives in San Diego, California, with her husband and two children. She is a pediatric nurse of more than two decades and a children's book author. Before her greatest adventure of motherhood, Sheri explored the country as a traveling nurse and enjoyed gallivanting the world, finally "finding herself" exactly where she was meant to be. For more about Sheri and her winding path to parenthood, visit www.youweremeantformebook.com or follow her on Instagram @youweremeantformebook.

The Waiting Room

SARAH ZIMMERMAN

When I was 14 weeks pregnant, I went to Disney World with my oldest sister's family and my parents. It was my first visit to the Magic Kingdom in more than two decades.

As an adult, I was less than enchanted with the experience. It was different from what I remembered. This time, the "magic" seemed forced, and the grandeur struck me as excessive. It seemed like everything was in caricature. But what left the biggest impression on me was the waiting. Oh, the waiting! Even with recent innovations like the Fast Pass and the handy Disney app, we waited hours for certain attractions. The newest and most popular rides had wait times of up to *four hours!* As a pregnant woman, I was thinking, "Can I make it this long without needing to sit down or use the toilet or get food and water?" The answer was, of course, no. What intrigued me, though, was that Disney had recognized that long waits could be problematic and created some of the most intricate and expensive holding rooms I've ever seen. For some rides, the waiting areas were almost more elaborate than the rides themselves.

So, it was easy to pass the time waiting. Waiting as a group was more enjoyable than waiting alone, and it was even better when we played a game together.

I may have been too harsh in my critique of Disney World. It does resemble real life in at least one way. So much of our life is spent waiting: to drive a car, to be able to vote, and to drink legally; to find our soulmate, to lose those extra 10 pounds, for our dream house to come on the market, for a positive pregnancy test result, for our baby to arrive. The wait for some of these milestones is tantamount to hell; pure torture. For other milestones, the wait can sometimes be alluring and meaningful. But often, when viewed against the entirety of one's lifetime, the "ride" at the end of the wait seems brief and anticlimactic. Ironically, what we often remember is the environment we experienced while waiting and the path (or paths) we took to get to the final destination, rather than the actual attraction for which we were waiting.

In the waiting area for the Peter Pan ride, a series of rooms represented the rooms in the Darling family house. You knew there was another room ahead, but if you were a novice anticipating the ride, you did not know which room would finally open into the actual ride. Some rooms were more interesting than others, but only one opened to the ride. This string of rooms is an apt analogy for my journey to motherhood: a journey of twists and turns, but nonetheless a meaningful journey that ultimately led me to my desired destination.

Down the Rabbit Hole

Cory and I married in June 2017 and almost immediately moved to Taipei, Taiwan, where he had accepted a job as a counselor and swimming coach at an international school. Cory was 33, and I was 30. We had known each other for almost a year and were excited to embark on this adventure. We both wanted children, but we thought it would be wise to wait at least a year before conceiving. We set aside age-related worries about conceiving so we could prioritize what we believed to be the bedrock of a healthy family: our marriage. My two older sisters had had several healthy pregnancies, and as a very health-conscious person, I was fairly certain conceiving would be simple for us when we were ready to try.

United States expatriates will tell you that one of the joys of living outside your home country is access to travel. And that rang true for us. Every school holiday we found ourselves traveling to another country or another part of the island.

The 2018 summer break coincided with our first wedding anniversary, which meant we could start trying to conceive while globetrotting. Our plan involved sleeping in 18 different beds across western Europe and the United States. I had never been to Europe, and I was excited to tour some of the places I'd only read about in books and seen in photos. I was particularly excited about the food and wine in France and Italy. I told my OBGYN that I wanted to try to conceive on the trip, and that I was concerned about how much wine I might drink in Europe. He laughed and said, "Don't worry, just have fun!" We toured London, Paris, Amsterdam, Florence, and Rome and loved every minute. We were completely carefree. I thought it would be so perfect to be able to say we had made a baby while on vacation in the French countryside. And I believed conceiving would really be that simple.

However, the vacation came and went without any sign of pregnancy. My periods came like clockwork, as always.

We returned to our normal routine and kept trying. We had not done anything special while trying during those blissful summer months: no thermometers, no pee strips, no recommended positions, no pills; just sex and an app that told me the peak times for conceiving.

In the fall, I started tracking my cycle more carefully. I began taking my temperature every morning and switched to a paid app to track my cycle and discern its patterns. After a few months, I started tracking my cervical mucus using the same app. It felt like a fascinating game in some ways, but then I always felt crushed when I sat on the toilet and saw blood. It was like I'd played the game and lost.

Around month four, I began searching on Google—my able ally one day and my arch-nemesis the next. Someone had once told me that you can find any answer you want through a Google search, and for me that statement proved true. I would spend time worrying about whether that exercise class I took made the potentially fertilized egg dislodge from the wall of my uterus, or whether I'd had one too many pieces of chocolate. Google was there to tell me it was my fault when I wanted to feel guilty, and it was there to relieve my fears when I wanted to feel like everything was going to be OK. It was there to tell me what to eat and drink and which foods to avoid. Some days, I would spend hours falling down the rabbit hole of fertility articles. This "game" I had begun was one I must win, a challenge I must conquer, and Google would help me accomplish it. Or so I thought.

A Companion on the Lonely Road

Meanwhile, a seed of loneliness planted itself deep inside me, telling me this problem was mine to fix because I was the woman. Merriam-Webster defines the word "barren" as "incapable of producing offspring—used especially for women or mating." I felt like I was in a waiting room, all alone. I was so careful! By this point I didn't drink any alcohol, nor did I consume caffeine. I was cautious not to exercise too vigorously after ovulation. I would note that my breasts felt particularly sore one day, or that I felt a little uneasy after eating something one morning, or that I had a few extra pimples on my face, and my hopes would rise, and Google would tell me that any or all of these things were "symptoms of pregnancy." I waited patiently until the 28th day of my cycle and noted every irregularity in my body, thinking they were all signs that I was pregnant. Then my period arrived like clockwork, and my hopes plummeted. It felt like a 28-day roller coaster.

Cory did not ride this roller coaster with me. He remained unaffected by the truths of nature. My period would come, and I would want to weep and wallow in my disappointment that another month had gone by fruitlessly. He would hug me and then move on to the next point of conversation as if it were no big deal. He and I discussed our trying to conceive one day, and when doing so I was reminded of a previous conversation we'd had about hope.

Hope manifests differently in everyone. Some of us are quicker than others to let hopes form inflexible expectations, and when we allow that to happen, our emotions become fiercely intertwined in the outcomes. Cory rarely (perhaps never) let hope become an expectation, and because of that, he was able to maintain a sense of steadiness when something he'd hoped for didn't come to fruition. Because his hope never transformed into an expectation, he didn't allow himself to get disappointed when something for which he hoped did not happen.

I believe in the power of hope. Later, my ability to hold on to hope was what allowed us to forge further along on our journey and ultimately arrive at our destination. But at this point in the story, it was Cory's skill of keeping his hopes in check that helped buoy me. At first, I hated that he never rode the emotional roller coaster with me, but once I was reminded of why, I decided to lean into him when the hills got too high and the valleys too low. I listened to him remind me of truths from scripture, which helped prevent me from being pulled down into the pit of despair each time my period started. I remembered that I had never been promised a child formed in my womb. I recalibrated so my desire to become a mother remained a hope, not an expectation. I allowed myself the joy of hope without getting caught up in the complication that comes with expectation. That doesn't mean I didn't occasionally get disappointed, but the feelings were much more palatable.

Cory was a rock for me, steady and unchanging. His love and presence helped steady me during the choppy emotional waves, but I still felt lonely for months. I felt like our childlessness was my fault, and according to Google, there are hundreds, if not thousands, of ways that I could try to fix our situation. Looking back, I can say with confidence that Google is not "someone" you want with you in life's waiting rooms. The truth is that according to the data, men are nearly equally likely to play a role in an infertility diagnosis, yet so much of the information about conception is geared toward women. This makes sense when you consider the fact that women are the ones carrying the burden of conceiving. I tracked my temperature every morning before getting out of bed, I checked my cervical mucus each day, I stayed in bed for 15 minutes after sex with my butt elevated and my knees curled up, I abstained from alcohol and caffeine and chocolate and possible listeria carriers for weeks on end, I calculated when and how often we should have sex. He had exactly one thing he had to do and the weight of my responsibilities seemed to be unfairly burdensome.

So, yes, the majority of steps to a baby involve the woman's body. And, wow, does it feel like a lonely one-sided journey! It doesn't help that people feel much more comfortable asking the woman, "When are you two planning to have children?" (A friendly piece of advice for everyone you know: don't ask that question or anything like it unless you know someone very well, and even then, second guess yourself.) About eight months into our trying, one of the parents of his swimmers asked me some variant of that question. After getting over the shock of hearing the question asked by a total stranger, I had to figure out how to respond gracefully while hiding the pang of despair that tore at my heart.

As we began planning our 2019 summer vacation, I started researching fertility specialists in Taipei. Although we had technically only been trying to conceive since late May 2018, I had been off of contraceptive pills since December 2017 and Cory had stopped using condoms around that time. I felt confident that we should begin the fertility testing process.

At some point during the preceding months, I had learned of the extremely low cost of in vitro fertilization (IVF) in Taiwan. I casually broached the subject with Cory one night at dinner. We ended up having a long and emotionally charged conversation. I had heard of IVF and knew many people who had successfully given birth to children through the process, but I knew very little about the science behind it. My husband, on the other hand, was much more familiar with the IVF process and what it entailed. We both believe life begins at the moment of conception, whether that conception happens internally or externally. The part of IVF I was unaware of was that the quantity of eggs fertilized (the number of embryos) typically exceeds (sometimes by a lot) the number of embryos implanted into a woman's uterus. So, it is not unusual for embryos to be created that the couple does not end up needing to use and this leaves a finite number of options for what to do with the surplus of embryos (that is, the embryos can be destroyed, donated to science, or donated to another couple or single individual). We weren't comfortable with the options. With this knowledge, I grew increasingly uncomfortable with the process. For us, no matter how inexpensive IVF was in Taiwan or how easy it was to access, we agreed that we would not choose to conceive this way.

Braving the Clinic

Although I had a regular OBGYN, we elected to go to a fertility clinic. I scheduled an appointment through its online portal using Google Translate.

It was an early morning appointment at an unfamiliar hospital, so I gave myself plenty of time to get there. The preceding night I had slept terribly, and the entire way there I was unaware of my surroundings, thinking of the weight of what I was going to do by seeing a fertility specialist. I was admitting we had a problem.

When I arrived, I had an incredibly difficult time navigating the hospital system due to both its bureaucracy and the language barrier. Finally, at the clinic, I was ushered in by nurses I had befuddled. Not only was I a white woman who didn't speak Mandarin, but I also had no medical record in the hospital system, and I had not been assigned an appointment for a specific doctor. I was eventually informed that I was in the wrong place—I had made an appointment at the clinic that handled the IVF process. Furthermore, I was told in broken English by the doctor on the floor that I could not see a fertility specialist until I had a record with an OBGYN affiliated with the hospital, indicating that I had been trying to conceive for more than a year.

Dismayed and determined not to be defeated, I went to the lobby and used the computer console to schedule an appointment with an OBGYN I selected at random from those with availability that day. I had no clue if this doctor would be male or female, and more importantly, whether he or she would speak enough English to understand my plight.

A few hours later, I had a well visit with an OBGYN. After ascertaining the reason I was there, she provided me with appropriate paperwork, prescriptions for tests, and a small container for Cory's contribution; she also recommended a fertility specialist and provided a card listing clinic times. Although the day had started with a lot of speed bumps, I ultimately made it to the desired outcome.

Over the next month, Cory and I both completed the fertility testing. There was a bit of an issue in understanding the instructions regarding the sperm collection and drop-off, which resulted in some situations one can do nothing but laugh about after the fact. I was thankful that my part of the testing process was fairly straightforward and unobtrusive. After we completed the tests, we made our appointment to receive the results at the next available time.

In Taiwan, patients are given a timeslot and a number, and the meeting with the doctor takes place at some point during the timeslot (and in numerical order). You wait right outside the specific doctor's office until your number flashes on the screen, at which point you go straight into a room to meet with the doctor. (A nurse will usually come out to obtain information before the patient's number is called.) Unlike my experiences in the United States, patients in Taiwan are not ushered to an empty exam room where they wait privately until the doctor finally knocks on the door. Of all the waiting room systems I have experienced during my life, I prefer the one in Taiwan the most. I am a planner by nature, and the Taiwanese system helps me know what to expect.

So, on a Tuesday evening in May, almost a year after we started trying to conceive, Cory and I sat in a waiting room outside a fertility specialist's office. Our appointment was for the 7 to 9 p.m. timeslot. Many of the other clinics were closed for the day, so the waiting area was dimly lit. We whiled away the time playing gin rummy.

Between the OBGYN appointment and fertility appointment, we had spent a fair amount of time discussing possible outcomes and processing the emotions surrounding them. One thing that unites us is faith in God, and we approach decision-making through the lens of our Christian faith. We trust that God is sovereign over all circumstances and that He knows all that has happened or will happen. As the weaver of a giant tapestry, He knows how all the threads fit together and weaves them to create a beautiful masterpiece, even when with our inferior human eyes we can only behold a small section of what to us might look off-putting. With these beliefs, we knew that whatever the result, we would accept it. We were comfortable with the idea of using science and technology to aid us in conception as long as the sperm met an egg (or eggs) inside my uterus.

We were also open to the idea of adoption but realistic in considering the extraordinary cost that can be associated with the process. We had also come to terms with the increasingly likely possibility that we would be barren and childless, yet we both still had hope.

Accordingly, there wasn't much to talk about as we waited. I remember remarking how thankful I was that Cory was with me in the waiting room. He was taken aback by that comment and said something along the lines of, "Of course I would be here! This is as much about me as it is about you." Looking back, I realize that statement—and what ensued during the following hours—revealed just how alone I'd felt in bearing the responsibility of our conception journey.

The nurse came out and collected my information, and we went into the claustrophobic room. I have walked into closets much larger than that room. There was only one chair by the doctor's desk. I sat down while Cory stood in the corner up against a cabinet.

I can't remember exactly what the fertility specialist said to kick off the conversation, but it was clear the conversation was not driven by knowledge of our test results. Her bedside manner was nonexistent, and the rapidity of her questions and assumed answers felt like a machine gun going off. She curtly told Cory to move aside so she could access the cabinet and pulled out a chart to show me how to track my basal body temperature for the next three months before sending that data to her to determine the date we should have sex. We looked at each other and then back at her incredulously, and I asked, "What about the test results? We're here to hear about our blood and semen test results." "Oh! You already take test?" The data in the computer stated all of this, if she had only read it. She opened our results and the following conversation transpired:

> Doctor: OK, your results are very normal, very good. Oh! His numbers are very low. Low count, low motility, and low morphology.
>
> Cory: What does this mean?
>
> Doctor: (Using a scrap of paper to write numbers to the tenth power and explaining in broken English) Numbers are too low to achieve conception. But you can do IVF.
>
> Cory: We are not interested in IVF, but what are the possibilities to conceive without it?
>
> Doctor: It would be a miracle.

If this conversation had been part of a sitcom the laugh track would have been playing because neither of us could understand that she was saying "miracle." She said it at least five times in the ensuing conversation, and it was only at the very end that we understood her. She spent the next five minutes trying to convince us to pursue IVF and wanting to understand our reasoning for why we would not, which was, frankly, none of her business. She ended the conversation with "I respect how you think, but you should think less."

For some reason, she also suggested I could get an ultrasound; maybe it was to tell where I was in my cycle. That required us to go back to the waiting room, take a number, wait for the ultrasound, and then return to her office.

In the waiting room, we were both processing what had just happened. Cory was very quiet. I followed suit. Cory has since described his experience of those moments to me, and it sounds like he experienced a mild form of shock. He describes a high-pitched ringing sound emanating from the lights, and he felt the ringing in his head so intensely as to block out all other noise and thoughts.

Meanwhile, I had been selfishly thinking, "I can't believe it's not me! At least I'm fine!" I had spent so many months thinking there was something I could do to fix the problem, and that the problem was mine to fix. I couldn't help but feel some relief. I turned to my fair-weather friend, Google, and discovered that low sperm count does not always equate with sterility and that there were, in fact, things one could do to attempt to alter the numbers. I shared this information with Cory, and he said, "Miracle, Sarah. She said it would be a miracle." Then we both waited in silence.

The ultrasound technician had no clue as to why I was on his table except that I was in an OBGYN clinic. Within seconds, he could see an egg in position for fertilization. He said, "Oh, good! Go home and do your homework!" I began silently weeping. With the next breath he said, "Oh, I see your husband's numbers are low. It's OK! You can do IUI!" I clarified that he was saying IUI (intrauterine insemination), not IVF, and it was as if a light had turned on. I stopped weeping. This man had just handed me a glimmer of real hope. Altering numbers as low as Cory's on our own seemed nigh impossible, but the fact that this technician had mentioned another option cast doubt on the fertility doctor's resolute response.

As I walked out of the room, I Googled IUI, and at that moment, Google worked to my benefit. I explained the situation to Cory and read the information on intrauterine inception aloud while we waited to be called back in to see the fertility doctor, and the ringing in his ears instantly stopped. We went back into the doctor's office armed with the knowledge that we were not without hope. She admitted that IUI was indeed another option, and we discussed the possibility and potential dates for pursuing the procedure. Interestingly, it was as if the doctor had magically remembered *all* the options.

A Simple Solution

She informed us that Cory's low sperm count could be a result of a treatable condition called a varicocele, which is similar to varicose veins, but in one's testicles. She wrote down the names of five urologists who could test and treat Cory. We left her office with a plan for how to make an appointment to pursue IUI for the egg that was in place. But her words were still discouraging, as she informed us that success would be unlikely if Cory's sperm morphology numbers did not improve.

On the cab ride home, we decided to pass on the opportunity to try IUI after weighing its costs and the low chances of success given Cory's current numbers.

In the following days, we talked about our options, and my Google searching turned to the male side of infertility. I purchased Lauren Manaker's book, *Fueling Male Fertility*. We were flying to the U.S. for summer vacation at the end of the week, so we were out of time to pursue the varicocele option. We decided to spend the summer following suggestions in the book and then visit a urologist upon our return to Taipei.

Cory's fertility plan included switching from briefs to boxers, eating a Mediterranean diet, restricting alcohol intake to wine in moderation except on the weekends, doing regular exercise (but not cycling), and pumping himself full of hundreds of dollars' worth of vitamins and supplements. For the most part, we stuck to the plan. We discussed our situation with many of our family and friends throughout the summer and garnered the prayers and support of a growing team of cheerleaders. Cory talked by phone with a friend who is a urologist. Off the record, his friend confirmed that a varicocele can be repaired, and that, in his experience, the treatment had led to naturally conceived children. The phone call was encouraging for Cory!

In the U.S., we tried to see a few urologists to determine whether Cory had a varicocele. But between our travel schedule and the wait to see most urologists, we were never able to see a doctor.

Back in Taiwan, we made an appointment with a urologist. I had shortlisted them based on proximity, perceived English ability, and scholarly papers published. We chose a teaching doctor who had published an article on male infertility relating to a varicocele in an English journal—no Google translating necessary.

At the end of July, there we were again, in another waiting room, quietly praying. This appointment felt as momentous as the one in May had. We would know whether Cory had a varicocele; if so, our chances would go up, and if not, our plans would switch to adoption.

Cory went in alone. The doctor, surrounded by a number of residents, felt his testicles and within seconds, declared that he had a varicocele. It was simple to fix, but they first needed to confirm that the surgery would not be in vain by first doing genetic testing (and a structural testicle and semen analysis).

Cory was visibly relieved. He gave me a giant hug, and, over my shoulder, I heard him whisper a prayer of thanksgiving. We both cried, encouraged by the hope that we might be able to conceive.

Within a few weeks, we came back to the doctor's office to go over Cory's test results. We went into the exam room together, and there were two chairs this time. The doctor confirmed that the low numbers were not due to a genetic predisposition, and the surgery was available if we wanted it. What a relief!

One thing I've learned from my journey to motherhood is that oftentimes obtaining an explanation for infertility can provide immense relief—perhaps even if the explanation is daunting. As humans, we do not like not knowing the reason for something. It is no surprise that the toddler years involve the constant refrain, "Why? Why mommy?" So, Cory and I both felt such relief the moment the doctor offered us the possibility of surgical repair of the varicocele. It was as if we'd finally arrived in the room that opened to the Peter Pan ride. We could see the ride in front of us, and our anticipation grew.

The surgery took place on September 2, 2019. I sat again in another waiting room, this time in one with approximately 50 other families. In this waiting room, the name of the patient was clearly displayed on the screen in the waiting room, along with the patient's current status. I could easily see Cory's name because his was the only one not written in Chinese characters. The font seemed huge next to the other names. A friend came and sat with me while I waited. We discussed normal things; it was as if we were having coffee on a normal Tuesday morning.

Meanwhile, Cory was in an operating room filled with residents watching a surgery that they rarely have the chance to see. My understanding is that a varicocele repair is rarely performed in Taiwan because it is common for Taiwanese to view not only pregnancy, but also the process of getting pregnant, as solely a female issue. And, therefore, male infertility is not a well-acknowledged concept in Taiwan. (And if it is, conception can easily occur at a cost.) My husband's surgery cost less than $1,000 and had the potential to yield abundant pregnancy opportunities. I'm glad those Taiwanese residents got to observe this uncommonly performed surgery.

Success at Last

We were told it takes approximately three months for new sperm to develop. In the middle of November, we visited Singapore for a weekend swim competition that turned into a job interview. We returned to Taiwan and immediately welcomed my parents for their annual Thanksgiving trip. The week included a tour of some of the island's magnificent natural wonders, a nontraditional Thanksgiving meal, a job offer, and a test strip indicating that I was ovulating.

Two weeks later, I felt fatigued during and after an exercise class. I chalked it up to too much wine the day before.

Day 28 of my cycle came and went with no sign of blood. My app told me I could be pregnant based on the ovulation and timing of sex, but it suggested I wait a few days before testing. In a few days, though, I'd be bound for Vietnam. So, I risked a false negative and tested my urine. Apparently, Cory's first batch of new sperm had just the right amount of everything. I was pregnant!

When Cory went to a follow-up appointment at the beginning of January, he waited patiently for his number to flash; he was bursting with joy and gratitude at the anticipation of telling the doctor that I was pregnant.

In August of 2020, in a world much different than the one in which he was conceived, Samuel made his long-awaited debut. During his time in the womb, we experienced many more periods of waiting. The COVID-19 pandemic ravaged the world around us and whether we could move to Singapore became uncertain. At week 30 of my pregnancy, after months of uncertainty as to where I would deliver and whether or not Singapore would allow us to enter due to COVID, we boarded a plane to our new home. Upon arriving in Singapore, we entered a two-week quarantine before being released into the general population. We waited for Samuel's arrival with joyful anticipation, and as of this writing, we wait with pangs of despair and longing for the time when we will finally be able to introduce him to his grandparents in the United States. We wait for the day life returns to the way it was before COVID. We are here waiting; the only difference is we wait this time as a family of three instead of a unit of two.

You may think that the moment you can hold your precious child in your arms, your waiting will end because your life is "complete." But it doesn't work that way—you just move to a new waiting room. The lessons I learned in the periods of stillness and anticipation are what helped me thrive in the next one. ■

SARAH ZIMMERMAN is an American ex-pat living in Singapore with her husband Cory and their son. Sarah previously worked in the events industry and as a private piano instructor in the Washington, D.C. metropolitan area. She enjoys exploring the world around her through food, music, and exercise. She despises small talk, but revels in developing deep and personal relationships (usually forged over a cup of coffee or a glass of good wine). You can contact Sarah at seyoung08@gmail.com.

Acknowledgments

Above all, I want to thank the eight women who were brave enough to share their moving stories with the world. Kelley, Molly, Janelle, Susie, Megan, Hannah, Sheri, and Sarah: it has been an honor to read your stories and witness the power each story holds.

Thank you to Mary-Forbes, who urged me to put words to paper and make this book a reality; and to Bob, Kate, Jim, Heath, my parents, and my editors Catherine and Rebecca, who each played an integral role in pushing me down the path to publication.

Finally, I have immense gratitude for Sarah Rose, who spoke the truth I needed to hear at the moment I needed to hear it; and to the many friends, acquaintances, family members, doctors and nurses, therapists, and acupuncturists—my village—who helped me cross over from the path *to* motherhood to the path *of* motherhood.

This page would also be incomplete without the acknowledgment of my three children. While they are not my motivation for writing it, if they were not here this book would not exist. I am beyond grateful to have been chosen to be their mother. These children are undoubtedly the children for whom I yearned and whom I was meant to mother.